Windows and Mirrors

Short Stories   Volume 1

Editor: Marilyn Chapman

Prentice-Hall Canada Inc., Scarborough, Ontario

For Ann Kelland—first encourager

Canadian Cataloguing in Publication Data

Main entry under title:

Windows and mirrors : short stories

ISBN 0-13-960485-5 (v. 1)

1. Readers—Short stories.   2. Readers (Secondary).
I. Chapman, Marilyn, date

PE1121.W55 1986   428.6   C85-099286-9

Accompanying Materials

Windows and Mirrors: Short Stories Volumes 1 and 2 and Teacher's
Guides

Prentice-Hall, Inc., Englewood Cliffs, New Jersey
Prentice-Hall International, Inc., London
Prentice-Hall of Australia, Pty., Ltd., Sydney
Prentice-Hall of India Pvt., Ltd., New Delhi
Prentice-Hall of Japan, Inc., Tokyo
Prentice-Hall of Southeast Asia (PTE) Ltd., Singapore
Editora Prentice-Hall do Brasil Ltda., Rio de Janeiro
Prentice-Hall Hispanoamericana, S.A., Mexico

3   4   5   6   D   91   90   89

Printed and bound in Canada by John Deyell Company

Project Editors: Iris Skeoch, Becky Vogan
Associate Editor: Catherine Leatherdale
Production: Monika Heike, Joanne Matthews
Series Design: Brian Bean
Composition: CompuScreen Typesetting Ltd.
Cover: Dresser and Dark Window by Christopher Pratt, 1981, oil on
   board. Collection: Ron Langstaffe. Courtesy Mira Godard Gallery.

Contents

Stories are listed alphabetically by author's last name. For alternate listings, see *Teacher's Guide*.

Preface

Windows and Mirrors is a two-volume anthology of Canadian short stories intended for secondary-school students across the country. The stories that appear in Volume 1 were selected to appeal to students with a wide range of abilities in grades nine and ten; the stories in Volume 2, to appeal to students with a wide range of abilities in grades eleven, twelve, and thirteen. Approximately four stories in each volume were selected to appeal to students in at least one of the following grade levels: general nines, advanced nines, general tens, advanced tens, general elevens, and so on. It is not assumed that all of the stories in either volume will be suitable for any *one* class.

All of the stories in Volume 2, and most of the stories in Volume 1, are written by authors who have produced at least one critically acclaimed volume of short stories. The main emphasis for the selection of stories in Volume 1 was on content appeal; the main emphasis for the selection of stories in Volume 2 was on literary excellence.

More than 1200 stories were read initially. From this number 110 were identified as "possibilities"; that is, their language and subject matter were appropriate for students at this level, their narratives were appealing, and the style in which they were written was representative of the author's work.

These "possibilities" were then narrowed down to 50 stories by applying the following criteria:

Were most of Canada's well-known short-fiction writers represented, along with a few promising new writers?

Were the stories teachable?

Were a variety of genres, styles, and tones represented?

Was there a reasonable representation of authors and protagonists of both sexes?

Were all of Canada's main geographical regions represented?

The final selections were made by a group of eleven students. Their only criterion: were the stories "a good read"?

The stories are arranged alphabetically by the author's last name in the text. Alternate arrangements may be found at the back of the *Teacher's Guide*.

Among those authors represented in Volume 2 of this series are Mavis Gallant, Sinclair Ross, Margaret Laurence, Gabrielle Roy, and Stephen Leacock.

Marilyn Chapman

Acknowledgments

With special thanks to Gayle Baxter, Lesley Cross, and Marie Gardner—sharp-eyed, gentle-tongued critics all. Thanks also to Ken Gardner, Diane Hummel, the English Department at Cameron Heights Collegiate (for assistance with the Glossary), and to student readers: Joy Barlow, Patrice Brown, Laura Dick, Michelle De Carlis, Carol DeVrieze, Chris Moser, Kelly Pineault, Shelley Rowe, Dave Spielmacher, Sonia Steeb, Wendy Veugen. My debt to these students is profound.

To Dorothy Greenaway, Iris Skeoch, Becky Vogan and Catherine Leatherdale of Prentice-Hall, my thanks for their enthusiasm and skilful editorial work.

To the Student

When we are at home looking through a window, we see, caught within the borders of the window's frame, a world that is different from our own. But if someone were suddenly to put silver nitrate on one side of this window, we'd see, within the frame of what has now become a mirror, ourselves and the world we inhabit. The one piece of glass has two possible functions: to show us others and to show us ourselves.

Some of the stories in this volume function as windows. They tell us about people and places we might otherwise have never encountered. They stretch our imaginations, making us wiser and more understanding.

Some of the other stories function as mirrors. When we read them, we see a world we recognize as our own. "Hey!" we say, "That's the kind of thing my mother does." Or, "There's a boy in my class who has hair like that." Or, "I remember a storm like that when I was a kid." In some ways these are the most satisfying stories of all because they articulate for us our own feelings, concerns, and perceptions.

Most stories, however, like our original piece of glass, have a double function: they give us both the privilege of seeing into someone else's world and the satisfaction of seeing into our own.

In order to get a window or mirror to reveal its secrets, all we need to do is open our eyes. To get a short story to do the same thing, we have to open not only our eyes but also our imaginations.

The results are always worth it.

The Dog Who Wanted to Die

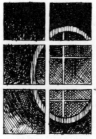 The Claphams rented the house next door to the Parkers the same week 15-year-old David Parker's father moved out. There had been some strange people renting there before, but the Claphams were the worst yet.

Mrs. Clapham was pale and tight lipped and rarely came out of the house. Mr. Clapham was large and red faced, and on weekends he rarely went into the house. Instead he bellowed and blustered and looked around the neighbourhood for things to complain about — children making too much noise, cars driving too fast, pets running loose. David thought this last complaint was ridiculous since the Claphams' own pet was always loose and was the biggest pest of all.

Just looking at their dog Monty made David sick. Though Monty's stomach was fat and bloated, his legs were spindly. His dull black fur was filled with crusts and scabs, and bald red patches with oozing sores.

The Claphams didn't seem to pay

COLLEEN
ARCHER

1

much attention to Monty. Now and then Mrs. Clapham would appear briefly on the back step and set down a bucket full of potato peelings, stale bread and leftover food. Monty would shuffle over to the bucket and eat the entire contents mechanically, as if under some obligation to reach the bottom.

The day after David's father left, Monty was lying on the Parkers' front lawn when David came home from school. The sight of the fat and smelly dog sent the boy into a rage.

"Get away!" he shouted, and stamped his feet. The dog blinked sadly and thumped his tail in dumb appeal. This made David even madder.

"I'm warning you, get moving."

He picked up a stone and raised his arm. The dog stared at the stone and cringed, but he still refused to budge. Then David, who had never deliberately hurt a living thing before, bounced the stone right off the side of the fat dog's head. With a yelp Monty heaved himself up and started slowly away, his tail between his legs and his sides heaving.

It was soon after this that David first noticed Monty's suicide attempts. Every time a car came into sight, Monty would head into the centre of the road and lie down on his side. Soon the neighbourhood became used to screeching brakes, angry shouts, and honking horns. Then there would be the roar of an engine as the driver would give up his futile attempt to rouse the dog and drive up the low curb in front of David's house.

Luck seemed to be with the dog (or perhaps not with him), for despite many close calls he survived day after day. During those days David's anger against his father grew and grew, but he got nowhere in his attempts to turn his mother against him.

"Why did he have to leave?" he would demand. "He had a good job here."

"It's not just a matter of a job," his mother would say quietly. "You know we decided to separate long before he got the supervisor offer. Please David, won't you at least drop him a line?"

Not only wouldn't David write to his father; he also burned the unopened letters postmarked "Ottawa" which came for him twice a week. Whenever his mother called him to the phone, he made sure before taking the receiver that it wasn't his father on the other end of the line.

Tiny Mrs. Parker worked harder than ever as a freelance photographer now she and David were alone. David, on the other hand, stopped working completely and his school marks dropped. His mother was afraid he might even fail his grade.

David came home from school one day in a mood as black as his hair to discover Monty sprawled in the centre of the street but not a car in sight. He picked up a stick and advanced towards the dog. Then he stopped as he noticed something unusual at the Claphams'. The curtains were gone from the windows and the lawn ornaments had disappeared from the yard. He went over to the house and peered through the living-room window. The room was bare.

"What're you doing?" It was Alvin Cross from the down the road. Alvin was a grade ahead of David at school.

"I'm looking for the Claphams."

"They moved away after lunch."

"But they can't have moved. Their dog's still here."

It didn't occur to David that people could go away and leave their pet behind.

"So call the Humane Society. They'll get rid of him for you."

"Get rid of him?"

"Sure. Who'd want a fat old mutt like that?"

Alvin went home and David was left alone, staring at the dog he loathed — the dog who asked nothing more than quick death. If he called the Humane Society, he reasoned, he'd be doing the dog a favour.

While he was thinking about this, a truck wheeled around the corner and headed towards them, going much too fast for a residential street. The driver saw Monty and stepped down hard on his brake. The truck screamed to a stop a few feet away from them.

"Get your dog off the road or I'll run right over him!" The driver began swearing at David and shaking his fist.

David knew exactly what he wanted to say. He wanted to say it wasn't his dog and to go right ahead and run over him. Then everybody would be happy. Instead he looked at the man's red face and the dog's limp body and something inside him stopped the words. He got down on one knee and held out his hand to Monty.

"Come here, boy."

Monty rose and tottered towards him, his tail making slow circles, his mouth open. When he reached David he licked the outstretched hand, but instead of responding with kindness the boy grabbed him by the fur on his neck and hauled him roughly into the house.

"How come you're bringing Monty in here?" asked David's mother. "I thought you didn't like him."

"The Claphams have moved out."

"Oh," said his mother, and that was all.

Although David had adopted Monty, his attitude towards him seemed unchanged. The dog followed him around, accepting any abuse with a slow wag of his tail and any small kindness with ecstasy. David's mother let him stay because she thought he might rouse David from his despair, but as time went on the boy's mood grew darker and darker.

Mrs. Parker worried constantly about him, but there seemed little she could do to help. She hated leaving him alone, but the insecurity of her job meant she had to teach a class at the community college Monday and Wednesday nights. One Wednesday she gathered her equipment as usual and headed out into the March darkness.

"Be sure to lock the door, David. You know how many robberies we've had on the street this month."

David didn't answer. By the time the old car roared away he was lying on his bed in the dark staring at the shadows.

His room was spartan by choice, with no posters and no loud colours. On the solid wooden desk, which had once been his father's, there was a microscope and a small aquarium. On the wall was a single shelf with a neat row of books — some science books, and a complete set of Black Stallion novels left over from his elementary school days.

Monty came in to keep him company, but David angrily ordered him out. Although Monty was now kept clean, he was still fat and covered with scabby patches and he made a sorry sight as he waddled dejectedly downstairs.

It must have been a half hour later when David realized there was someone in the house. He could hear drawers being opened in the dining-room, and every few seconds an eerie beam of light played on the hall wall. David felt like his heart had stopped. Why hadn't he locked the door? Why hadn't he left some lights on?

Then there were footsteps on the stairs, and David felt certain he was going to faint. In the dark he couldn't even find anything to use as a weapon. Maybe if he lay very still everything would be all right.

Suddenly a large figure stood framed in the doorway. The flashlight circled the room, and stopped right on David's face.

David was too terrified to scream, and his eyes closed in terror as the arm with the flashlight descended towards his head. There was no pain, however. Instead he heard a low snarl, and when he opened his eyes, Monty was clinging tightly to the jacketed arm. Next David heard swearing, and he saw Monty drop to the floor and a leg kick out. There was a scuffling sound, and then silence.

By the time David was calm enough to turn on the lights and call the police, the man was gone. Mrs. Parker's silverware lay scattered in the hall and Monty was on his side on the floor, panting heavily and obviously in pain.

It was two kindly police officers who drove David and Monty to the vet's and David told them his story on the way. He hadn't seen the man's face, but the police found hair and fibre samples in Monty's fur, which months later would help them convict a suspect.

The police had contacted Mrs. Parker and she was on her way to the vet's office. Meanwhile David sat on a chair next to the examining table with tears in his eyes.

"What's wrong with him, Doctor? Is he going to die?"

The young vet smiled comfortingly. "Just bruised ribs. They'll be better soon." Then her smile disappeared.

"His general condition is something else. What have you been feeding him?"

"He wasn't my dog until a little while ago!" said David indignantly. "He was fat and old when I got him."

"He's not old, David. He's probably four at the most. He's just a victim of neglect."

David was suddenly humble.

"What can I do for him, Doctor? Can I make him better?"

"You can, but are you sure you want to take it on? It will be a big job, you know."

"What do I do, please?"

"First, here's a powder for the infections on his skin. He also has eczema, so give him cod liver oil every day. And no starch. Dogs have a short digestive tract and they need a concentrated diet. Then there's grooming and exercise. See that he gets plenty of exercise. Now I'm going to give him a couple of needles to protect him against disease, and then you'd better both get home to bed."

Mr. Parker had always said that once David got started on something there was no stopping him. Over the next few months Mrs. Parker couldn't believe she was living with the same boy she had known right after Mr. Parker left. David was up every morning at 6 taking Monty for a two-mile walk. At first the dog moved slowly, but gradually he was able to walk quickly, then trot, and finally run.

Each day after school David groomed Monty. He removed all the mats from Monty's hair with a thinning shears, then he brushed him. For the first few weeks the brushing and combing had to be done very gently because of the sores, but after a month the sores had healed and Monty's coat was shining and soft.

As for food, David watched Monty's diet more closely than his own. Besides oil and rationed kibble and meat, Monty also got hard biscuits to clean his teeth, beefhide strips, and raw rounded soup bones.

All this care cost money, and David knew he should earn it himself instead of relying on his mother. After a lot of searching he found a job delivering circulars for the community's advertising paper. It wasn't much of a job, but it was enough to keep Monty, with a little spending money left over for himself.

When June came, David rushed home with his report card and handed it to his mother.

"Passed with honours," his mother read, and she hugged him proudly. "Come on David, let's go out for dinner and celebrate!"

That same night they were watching a television show when the phone rang.

"David." Mrs. Parker's voice was hesitant, her eyes pleading. "It's for you. It's your dad."

To her surprise, David came forward and took the receiver.

"Hello, Dad? How are you?" At first David's voice was shy. Then suddenly the words poured out.

"I'm coming to visit you this summer after all. I'll be down on the bus next week. Only for a few days, though. I can't leave my dog for long. I'll have to tell you all about Monty, Dad. He's the best looking dog you've ever seen. Did Mum tell you he probably saved my life?"

David was so busy talking he didn't see his mother smile. Nor did he hear the thump of a well brushed tail on the hard kitchen floor as he spoke the name "Monty" in a voice filled with love.

The Heroine of Lunenburg

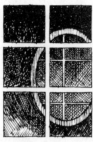 Sixteen-year-old Sylvia posed, tall and slim, with skin as black and smooth as polished ebony, in front of the fine mirror in her master's parlour. She couldn't help smiling at her own reflection, dressed as she was in the beautiful green silk gown, embroidered with golden braid. She dropped herself a curtsey and spun round on her tiptoes. The great skirt billowed out like the sails of a ship in a stiffening breeze. Clapping her hands, she laughed aloud with pleasure.

With that, she heard the sound of heavy footsteps and a wheezy voice exclaimed, "What's going on? Where did you get that gown?"

She whirled to face the short, stout woman who had just entered the room followed by a small, fair-haired boy.

"It's mine, Missy Smith! The gown is mine! Mistress Creighton gave it to me afore she died."

"You're a thief, you lying wench," Mistress Smith wheezed, her pale skin blotching red and her tiny, pig-like eyes blazing with anger.

JOYCE
BARKHOUSE

"Sylvie's not a liar! My mamma did give her the green dress!" shouted the boy as he ran to Sylvia's side. "And she's not a wench either," he added angrily.

"She's a black slave, that's what she is, and she's no business in the parlour," retorted the fat woman.

The child stamped his foot and raised his fist.

"I hate you!" he cried, bursting into tears.

"That's enough! Come along at once, Master Timmy! As for you, Sylvia, get back downstairs to the kitchen where you belong. Colonel Creighton shall hear about this when he gets home."

Wheezing heavily, Mistress Smith seized Timmy by the arm and dragged him howling from the room. For a moment, Sylvia stayed defiantly where she was. Then, instead of going to the kitchen, she slipped outside into the garden and ran to a favourite corner by the picket fence where she was completely hidden from the house by a clump of lilac bushes. For a long time she remained there, sad and brooding.

The home of Colonel Creighton stood on the slope of a steep hill overlooking Lunenburg Harbour, on the south shore of Nova Scotia. From her hiding place, Sylvia could see down over the roofs of the closely clustered houses to the harbour itself. It was empty on that day, for the men of the town had set sail for deep-sea fishing off the Grand Banks of Newfoundland.

A shiver ran through her and, suddenly, she felt a strange sense of foreboding. It was midsummer of the year 1782: a year when England was at war with her rebellious colonies to the south; and no Nova Scotian coastal settlement was ever entirely safe from the looting, pillaging and burning of Yankee privateers. She directed her eyes away from the harbour and out to sea. There were no ships there either. All seemed safe.

"It's just 'cos I'm upset, seeing Timmy crying all the time and not being able to go and comfort him," she decided, pushing the feeling aside and turning to peer through the lilacs at the house.

"Missy Creighton wouldn't like what's happening," she murmured regretfully, "not to Timmy or me."

Her mind went back over how much things had changed since Mrs. Creighton's death, and especially since Timmy's fifth birthday a few months ago.

"He needs a governess," Colonel Creighton had announced then. "Someone to teach him his lessons and proper manners."

The choice of Mistress Smith to fill the post had not been a happy one. Unfortunately, English-speaking servants willing to work in an outpost like Lunenburg were hard to find because, except for the Colonel and his household and the handful of soldiers at the blockhouse, almost all of the town's other inhabitants were German-speaking.

"Wish I could have taught Timmy to read and write and cipher," Sylvia thought, but like most slaves she had in fact been denied all opportunity to learn these things herself.

She looked again at the flowing skirt and smoothed the lovely material with her two hands. Tears came to her eyes as she remembered the morning her invalided mistress had called her to her bedside.

"You'll never know how pleased I am I brought you with me from my parents' home when I married and came north," Mrs. Creighton had said gently. "You're the best friend I've had in this wild country, and I know Timmy will never want for mothering as long as you're with him. I want you to choose one of my party dresses and keep it for your own. Perhaps, sometimes, you could dress up in it, just for fun."

At first, Sylvia had been reluctant to obey but now she was glad she had. What a comfort it was to her, having just this one thing left from those happier times!

She smoothed the dress again. "I must change and get back to work," she thought. But when she reached the lean-to which served as her sleeping and dressing room, she found her bundle of garments had disappeared.

She hurried into the kitchen. Mistress Smith was there,

poking at something in the fireplace. A rank odour filled the air.

"What are you doing?" asked Sylvia in dismay, as she recognized the smell of burning cloth.

"Since you have such a fine gown, I thought you'd have no need of your old rags. I've burned them," came the reply.

"But that's wicked! I have no other clothes!" cried Sylvia.

"Then you'll just have to wear what you have on, won't you?" Mistress Smith said, with a cruel smile, as she left the room.

Bitterly, Sylvia went about her evening tasks. She tried to move carefully around the small kitchen but she was hampered by the great billowing skirt. She brushed it against the greasy edge of the slab table, spattered gravy on it from the roast and dipped the hem into the hot ashes as she lifted the kettle from the hob. Already the gown — the only beautiful thing she had ever owned — was ruined.

That night she cried herself to sleep. She slept uneasily, awakening before anyone else was about to hear the first cock crow in the early dawn. Immediately, her thoughts turned to what she could wear. She thought of going to Colonel Creighton for help, but she knew it would be of little use. Mistress Smith would already have given him her version of the story. In desperation, she tried wrapping herself in the blanket which covered her straw mattress, but she realized at once she could never clutch it about her as she worked. Sorrowfully, she pulled on the soiled green dress again.

She built up the fire in the kitchen, carried water from the well and set it to boil. Next she had to go to the far pasture with the milking stool and bucket to milk the cows. Getting away from the house felt good. For a little while she could pretend she was free, free as the white gulls that swooped and soared over the sea.

As she walked high up on the hill though she felt again the same unease she had known the previous evening. This time she made no attempt to put it from her but instead breathed deeply, moving her head from side to side. Could there be a bear or wildcat among the cattle, she wondered? But no, her sixth sense told her that if indeed there were danger about, it came from elsewhere.

She stopped to stand and listen. A song sparrow trilled and a whiff of wood smoke mixed with the sweet perfume of wild roses came to her. Then somehow the world seemed unnaturally still. She entered the pasture. Now she was sure there was something wrong. The cattle had stopped in their grazing. Every one of them was staring out towards the sea. She followed their gaze.

Down in the harbour a boat was coming swiftly to shore as men bent strongly to the oars. Beyond it, a tall vessel rode at anchor. The banner at the vessel's masthead was not the Jack of England. Privateers!

Clutching stool and bucket, kicking at the green dress as it caught and twisted round her legs, Sylvia raced down the hill.

"Master! The Yankees are coming!" she gasped, as she burst into the house where the family sat at breakfast.

Colonel Creighton strode to the window. "Get my gun from the kitchen. I must go to the blockhouse," he ordered sharply, as he buckled on his sword.

Sylvia obeyed, and then stood in the doorway to watch her master go. Even as she watched, armed men came rushing up the hill and the first shot was fired. Behind her, Mistress Smith uttered a wild scream. Numb with shock, Sylvia could neither move nor think till Timmy pushed past her and ran outside.

"No! No, Timmy," she cried.

A warning bullet whistled past her head. Forgetting all else she ran down the steps, gathered the boy in her arms and threw herself on the ground, shielding his body with her own. Moments later she looked up and saw that men were smashing windows and doors in a nearby house.

"Let us in! Or we'll set your place afire!" they shouted.

A woman yelled something back at them in German. Sylvia's mind began to work again.

"Hush, Timmy," she whispered. "Don't cry. We must try to save what we can."

Her dress was torn now and covered in dust but she gave it no thought. Gathering up the skirts as best she could and taking Timmy's hand, she went back into the house and snatched her empty milk bucket from the floor.

"Stay here, Tim," she said, pushing the little boy under a table for safety.

Mistress Smith and the other servants had disappeared. Alone then, Sylvia fetched Colonel Creighton's strong box. She dropped it inside the bucket and carried it outside. To her relief no one was watching. Quickly, she lowered the bucket into the well and hurried back to the house.

All around now, the town was in an uproar. People were streaming out of their homes towards the surrounding woods, some running empty-handed, others staggering under pieces of furniture. Sounds of gunfire came from the blockhouse.

Timmy had stayed under the table. "Come on, now. Let's get the chest of silver outside," Sylvia said.

She had dragged the heavy box only halfway across the garden, when a group of privateers came around the corner of the house. Quick as a flash she saw that she could profit now from Mistress Smith's cruelty of the day before. Holding Timmy in her arms, she sank down, covering the chest with her flowing skirts. One of the men went up to her.

"Why haven't you run off to the woods with the others?" he roared.

Seizing her by one arm he yanked at her viciously. She resisted, screaming at the top of her lungs. Terrified, Timmy pounded at the privateer with his fists.

"Leave her alone! Leave her alone!" he cried.

Another man joined them. "Orders have just been issued not to burn any more buildings," he directed. "Get what valuables you can from here and move on."

The men left. Sylvia dragged the chest across the grassy lawn and hid it in the lilacs. Then, at last, she and Timmy ran up the hill and through the pasture to the shelter of the forest.

Before dark the privateers sailed away. From her lookout, Sylvia could see that Colonel Creighton's house remained standing, and nearly all the fires had burned low.

"Come on, Timmy. Let's go home," she said.

That night, she slept alone in the house with Timmy in her arms.

"Don't be afraid," she comforted him.

"I'm not scared when I'm with you, Sylvia," he whispered. "But where is Papa?"

"I don't know," she had to say.

Others came back to the ruined town next day, but Colonel Creighton did not return. When a relief ship sailed in, days later from Halifax, Sylvia learned that he and two other men had given themselves up as hostages to prevent the whole town being razed.

Mistress Smith took ship at once for Halifax. The other servants followed her example but Sylvia refused to leave. Since no one else seemed to care about Timmy, she kept him with her.

It was the beginning of a free and happy time for both of them. They picked wild berries and gathered nuts. They had milk in plenty, some of which Sylvia made into butter and cheese. The hens laid well so there were eggs to trade and sell as well as to eat. What's more, Sylvia made friends with some neighbouring Micmac Indians. They brought gifts of meat — hare and partridge and venison — in return for loaves of bread and scalding hot cups of strong tea.

Colonel Creighton knew none of this. When, in 1783 at the end of the war, he was released, no one could tell him what had become of his only son. Brokenhearted and believing himself to be ruined, he returned to Lunenburg simply to salvage what he could. As he climbed the hill, he was both surprised and angry to see smoke rising from the chimney of his home.

"Squatters!" he thought. "Someone has moved in, thinking I'd never come back."

When he opened the door, though, he was greeted by a glad cry. Timmy, rosy-cheeked and well, threw himself into his father's arms. Stunned with surprise, the Colonel looked up to see Sylvia's welcoming smile.

"I . . . I can't believe it," he said, tears of gratitude filling his eyes.

It was Timmy who told the story of Sylvia's courage, and who showed his father where the strong box and chest of silver had been buried behind the lilac bushes in the garden. Everything was there, down to the smallest coin. As Colonel Creighton again tried to express his thanks, Sylvia grinned.

"It was lucky, after all, I was wearing Missy Creighton's green gown. Remember? My own skimpy skirt would never have covered that chest," she said.

Somewhat ashamed, she looked down at the ragged makeshift dress she had sewed together from scraps of cloth.

"You'll never want for proper clothing again," Colonel Creighton declared indignantly. "Tomorrow we pack and get ready to return to Halifax, for I'm no longer posted here."

And so it was that Sylvia left Lunenburg for good. For a few years she remained with Colonel Creighton and Timmy, but it was of her own choice, for the Colonel wasted no time in signing legal papers which freed her from slavery.

In Halifax, she met and fell in love with another freed slave. They were married and there the record of Sylvia's life ends. It is, however, likely that she and her husband settled in one of Nova Scotia's Black Loyalist communities. Certainly the story of her strength and loyalty, her honesty and courage should live on forever.

Very Special Shoes

All winter eleven-year-old Mary Johnson had been dreaming of a pair of red leather shoes she had seen in a shoe-store window on the avenue one afternoon when she was out with her mother doing the shopping. Every Saturday she had been given twenty-five cents for doing the housework all by herself and the day had come at last when it added up to six dollars, the price of the shoes. Moving around the house very quietly so she would not wake her mother who seemed to need a lot of sleep these days, Mary finished up the last of the dusting and hurried to the window and looked out: on such a day she had been afraid it might rain but the street was bright in the afternoon sunlight. Then she went quickly into the bedroom where her mother slept, with one light cover thrown half over her. "Mother, wake up," she whispered excitedly.

Mrs. Johnson, a handsome woman of fifty with a plump figure and a high colour in her cheeks, was lying on her left side with her right arm hanging loosely over the side of the bed: her mouth was open a little, but she was breathing so

MORLEY
CALLAGHAN

softly Mary could hardly hear her. Every day now she seemed to need more sleep, a fact which worried Mary's older sisters, Barbara and Helen, and was the subject of their long whispering conversations in their bedroom at night. It seemed to trouble Mr. Johnson too, for he had started taking long walks by himself and he came home with his breath smelling of whiskey. But to Mary her mother looked as lovely and as healthy as ever. "Mother," she called again. She reached over and gave her shoulder a little shake, and then watched her mother's face eagerly when she opened her eyes to see if she had remembered about the shoes.

When her mother, still half asleep, only murmured, "Bring me my purse, Mary, and we'll have our little treat," Mary was not disappointed. She gleefully kept her secret. She took the dime her mother gave her and went up to the store to get the two ice-cream cones, just as she did on other days, only it seemed that she could already see herself coming down the street in the red leather shoes: she seemed to pass herself on the street, wearing the outfit she had planned to wear with the shoes, a red hat and a blue dress. By the time she got back to the house she had eaten most of her own cone. It was always like that. But then she sat down at the end of the kitchen table to enjoy herself watching her mother eat her share of the ice-cream. It was like watching a big eager girl. Mrs. Johnson sat down, spread her legs, and sighed with pleasure and licked the ice-cream softly and smiled with satisfaction and her mouth looked beautiful. And then when she was finished and was wiping her fingers with her apron Mary blurted out, "Are we going to get my shoes now, Mother?"

"Shoes. What shoes?" Mrs. Johnson asked.

"The red leather shoes I've been saving for," Mary said, looking puzzled. "The ones we saw in the window that we talked about."

"Oh. Oh, I see," Mrs. Johnson said slowly as if she hadn't thought of those particular shoes since that day months ago.

"Why, Mary, have you been thinking of those shoes all this time?" And then as Mary only kept looking up at her she went on fretfully, "Why, I told you at the time, child, that your father was in debt and we couldn't afford such shoes."

"I've got the six dollars saved, haven't I? Today."

"Well, your father . . ."

"It's my six dollars, isn't it?"

"Mary, darling, listen. Those shoes are far too old for a little girl like you."

"I'm twelve next month. You know I am."

"Shoes like that are no good for running around, Mary. A pair of good serviceable shoes is what you need, Mary."

"I can wear them on Sunday, can't I?"

"Look, Mary," her mother tried to reason with her, "I know I said I'd get you a pair of shoes. But a good pair of shoes. Proper shoes. Your father is going to have a lot more expense soon. Why, he'd drop dead if he found I'd paid six dollars for a pair of red leather shoes for you."

"You promised I could save the money," Mary whispered. And then when she saw that worried, unyielding expression on her mother's face she knew she was not going to get the shoes; she turned away and ran into the bedroom and threw herself on the bed and pulled the pillow over her face and started to cry. Never in her life had she wanted anything as much as she wanted the red shoes. When she heard the sound of her mother moving pots and pans in the kitchen she felt that she had been cheated deliberately.

It began to get dark and she was still crying, and then she heard her mother's slow step coming toward the bedroom. "Mary, listen to me," she said, her voice almost rough as she reached down and shook Mary. "Get up and wipe your face, do you hear?" She had her own hat and coat on. "We're going to get those shoes right now," she said.

"You said I couldn't get them," Mary said.

"Don't argue with me," her mother said. She sounded blunt and grim and somehow far away from Mary. "I want you to get them. I say you're going to. Come on."

Mary got up and wiped her face, and on the way up to the store her mother's grim, silent determination made her feel lonely and guilty. They bought a pair of red leather shoes. As Mary walked up and down in them on the store carpet her mother watched her, unsmiling and resolute. Coming back home Mary longed for her mother to speak to her, but Mrs. Johnson, holding Mary's hand tight, walked along, looking straight ahead.

"Now if only your father doesn't make a fuss," Mrs. Johnson said when they were standing together in the hall, listening. From the living-room came the sound of a rustled newspaper. Mr. Johnson, who worked in a publishing house, was home. In the last few months Mary had grown afraid of her father: she did not understand why he had become so moody and short-tempered. As her mother, standing there, hesitated nervously, Mary began to get scared. "Go on into the bedroom," Mrs. Johnson whispered to her. She followed Mary and had her sit down on the bed and she knelt down and put the red shoes on Mary's feet. It was a strangely solemn, secret little ceremony. Mrs. Johnson's breathing was heavy and laboured as she straightened up. "Now don't you come in until I call you," she warned Mary.

But Mary tiptoed into the kitchen and her heart was pounding as she tried to listen. For a while she heard only the sound of her mother's quiet voice, and then suddenly her father cried angrily, "Are you serious? Money for luxuries at a time like this!" His voice became explosive. "Are we going crazy? You'll take them back, do you hear?" But her mother's voice flowed on, the one quiet voice, slow and even. Then there was a long and strange silence. "Mary, come here," her father suddenly called.

"Come on and show your father your shoes, Mary," her mother urged her.

The new shoes squeaked as Mary went into the living-room and they felt like heavy weights that might prevent her from fleeing from her father's wrath. Her father was sitting at the little table by the light and Mary watched his face desperately to see if the big vein at the side of his head had started to swell. As he turned slowly to her and fumbled with his glasses a wild hope shone in Mary's scared brown eyes.

Her father did not seem to be looking at her shoes. With a kind of pain in his eyes he was looking steadily at her as if he had never really been aware of her before. "They're fine shoes, aren't they?" he asked.

"Can I keep them? Can I really?" Mary asked breathlessly.

"Why, sure you can," he said quietly.

Shouting with joy Mary skipped out of the room and along the hall, for she had heard her sisters come in. "Look, Barbara, look, Helen," she cried. Her two older sisters, who were stenographers, and a bit prim, were slightly scandalized. "Why, they're far too old for you," Barbara said. "Get out, get out," Mary laughed. "Mother knows better than you do." Then she went out to the kitchen to help her mother with the dinner and watch her face steadily with a kind of rapt wonder, as if she was trying to understand the strange power her mother possessed that could make an angry man like her father suddenly gentle and quiet.

Mary intended to wear the shoes to church that Sunday, but it rained, so she put them back in the box and decided to wait a week. But in the middle of the week her father told her that her mother was going to the hospital for an operation.

"Is it for the pains in her legs?" Mary asked.

"Well, you see, Mary, if everything comes off all right," her father answered, "she may not have any pains at all."

It was to be an operation for cancer, and the doctor said the operation was successful. But Mrs. Johnson died under the anaesthetic. The two older sisters and Mr. Johnson kept repeating dumbly to the doctor, "But she looked all right. She looked fine." Then they all went home. They seemed to huddle first in one room then in another. They took turns trying to comfort Mary, but no one could console her.

In the preparations for the funeral they were all busy for a while because the older sisters were arranging for everyone to have the proper clothes for mourning. The new blue dress that Helen, the fair–haired one, had bought only a few weeks ago, was sent to the cleaners to be dyed black, and of course Mary had to have a black dress and black stockings too. On the night when they were arranging these things Mary suddenly blurted out, "I'm going to wear my red shoes."

"Have some sense, Mary. That would be terrible," Helen said.

"You can't wear red shoes," Barbara said crossly.

"Yes, I can," Mary said stubbornly. "Mother wanted me to wear them. I know she did. I know why she bought them." She was confronting them all with her fists clenched desperately.

"For heaven's sake, tell her she can't do a thing like that," Helen said irritably to Mr. Johnson. Yet he only shook his head, looking at Mary with that same gentle, puzzled expression he had had on his face the night his wife had talked to him about the shoes. "I kind of think Mary's right," he began, rubbing his hand slowly over his face.

"Red shoes. Good Lord, it would be terrible," said Helen, now outraged.

"You'd think we'd all want to be proper," Barbara agreed.

"Proper. It would be simply terrible, I tell you. It would look as if we had no respect."

"Well, I guess that's right. All the relatives will be here," Mr. Johnson agreed reluctantly. Then he turned hopefully to Mary. "Look, Mary," he began. "If you get the shoes dyed you can wear them to the funeral and then you'll be able to wear them to school every day too. How about it?"

But it had frightened Mary to think that anyone might say she hadn't shown the proper respect for her mother. She got the red shoes and handed them to her father that he might take them up to the shoemaker. As her father took the box from her, he fumbled with a few apologetic words. "It's just what people might say. Do you see, Mary?" he asked.

When the shoes, now dyed black, were returned to Mary the next day she put them on slowly, and then she put her feet together and looked at the shoes a long time. They were no longer the beautiful red shoes, and yet as she stared at them, solemn-faced, she suddenly felt a strange kind of secret joy, a feeling of certainty that her mother had got the shoes so that she might understand at this time that she still had her special blessing and protection.

At the funeral the shoes hurt Mary's feet for they were new and hadn't been worn. Yet she was fiercely glad that she had them on. After that she wore them every day. Of course now that they were black they were not noticed by other children. But she was very careful with them. Every night she polished them up and looked at them and was touched again by that secret joy. She wanted them to last a long time.

The Father

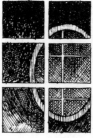 It wasn't the boy who gave him the invitation, but the boy's mother, his wife. Somehow even a little thing like this had become a shameful chore that the boy had avoided. Over the past year or two father and son had drifted apart, so that a strange shame and embarrassment coloured every event that brought them into contact.

His wife had waited until the children had gone out after supper, the boy to play baseball and his older sister to run and scream with other teen-agers in the schoolyard. Then she had said, "Johnny wonders if you'll go to the Boy Scout meeting with him tomorrow night?"

It was on the tip of his tongue to say, "Scout meeting! What do I look like?" Instead he asked, "Why, what's on there?"

"It's a father-and-son banquet," she said.

"Why didn't Johnny ask me to go?"

"You know he is — I guess he was too shy," she answered.

"Too shy! Too shy to ask his own father to go somewhere?"

"Well, I guess he was afraid you'd say no," she said.

HUGH
GARNER

23

"I'll think it over," he said grudgingly, knowing that he owed it to the boy, and also feeling that it might be a way of overcoming the barrier that had sprung up between them.

He didn't look forward to an evening spent in the company of a bunch of professional fathers, who were "real pals" to their sons. He had seen them making a nuisance of themselves, unable or unwilling to let their kids lead their own lives. They went swimming with their children, tried to umpire their ball games, and wrongly explained the displays at the museum and the animals at the zoo. He wouldn't normally mix with such men, but it was probably a big event for the boy, and it only happened once a year.

He poured himself a small drink and sat before the TV set, thinking of the coolness between him and his son and trying vainly to pinpoint its beginning. He knew that most of the time he was too preoccupied with other things to pay much heed to the boy's activities, but he had dismissed his misgivings with the thought, "He's only a twelve-year-old who wants to be left alone."

Over his drink he remembered the times he had been too harsh with the boy, and the times he had been curt and impatient. And with a feeling of angry revulsion he remembered siding with the teacher when he had been called to the school to discuss the boy's bad marks in reading. The principal had intimated that the boy's slowness might be caused by tensions in the home, but this he had vehemently denied. When the teacher had suggested keeping the boy in the same grade for a second year, he had acquiesced willingly, wanting only to get away from the place. The boy had looked up at him, bitten his lower lip, and had left the principal's office. From then on their distance one from the other was greater than ever.

On the evening of the banquet he was a little late getting home, having stopped in for a few drinks with a customer who was buying an industrial site. He ate warmed-over supper by himself, insisting all the while to his wife that there was no use eating when he was going to a banquet.

"You'd better eat," she said. "You've got to be at your best tonight."

"I'll be at my best, don't worry. I have a couple of drinks with a customer, and you're ready to shove me in an institution."

After he had bathed and shaved he put on his best suit. Though he had only contempt for scoutmasters he was anxious to create a good impression for the sake of the boy. His suits were getting tight, as were the collars of his shirts. It was sitting at a desk all day did it, and not walking anywhere any more. At the end of the war he had been lean and tough, but now he was middle-aged, fat, with his hair thinning fast on top.

He went downstairs and waited in the living room for the boy. The food his wife had pushed on to him had destroyed the glow from the pre-dinner drinks, so he poured himself a tall one for the road. From upstairs came the sound of his wife and son having their usual spat about the boy combing his hair. Though his wife and children quarrelled often, there was no tension between them at all.

The boy came down, wearing a pair of flannels and a blazer.

"Where's your scout uniform, Johnny?" he asked.

"We don't have to wear it if we don't want to," the boy said.

"I'll bet most of the other kids'll be wearing theirs."

The little boy shrugged.

His wife said, "Leave him alone, John. The reason he isn't wearing his uniform is that he only has half of it."

He couldn't remember how the boy had been dressed on scout night.

"Why hasn't he got the whole thing?" he asked his wife angrily. "We're not on the welfare, are we? Surely we could spend a few dollars for a complete scout uniform."

"Yes, but after you bought him the hockey pads and the rifle last Christmas he was afraid to ask you for anything else. He has the pants, belt and shirt, and all he needs is the neckerchief — "

"Afraid to ask me! That's all I hear around this place.

What's the matter with this family anyway? God knows what the neighbours must think of me."

"There's no use getting angry," his wife said. "He'll have the whole uniform before long. He doesn't really need it tonight."

"Jimmy Agnew and Don Robertson aren't going to wear their uniform," the boy said, trying to mollify him.

He wondered angrily if the scoutmaster thought he was too cheap to buy the boy a uniform. Probably he said to his assistants, "It's too bad about little Johnny Purcell, isn't it? There's a kid been coming here for four months now and he still hasn't got a uniform." He felt a twinge of indigestion as he pictured the scoutmasters — a couple of big sissies running around in short pants playing woodsmen.

He said to his wife, "Listen, Helen, for God's sake take him downtown with you tomorrow and get the rest of the Boy Scout outfit. I don't want those goons down at the church thinking I'm too cheap to buy him one."

He expected the boy's face to light up at this, but he stood in the doorway wearing a blank expression. It was the same look the boy put on when he and his wife quarrelled, or when he had too much to drink and tried to talk to the kid man to man.

When they left the house his daughter shouted after them, "Thank goodness we're getting rid of the men for the rest of the evening," and she and her mother laughed. The remark irritated him by pointing up the infrequency of such occasions.

As they walked down the street he felt a warm pride as he stole glances down at the boy. Everyone said the youngster was the spit and image of himself when he was younger, and they both bore the same first name. Fatherhood was the rounding out of a life, probably what was meant in the Bible by a person having to be born again. But even as he thought these things he knew it was only a fuzzy sentimentality brought on by what he had drunk.

The boy strode along beside him, his hands shoved deep into his pockets, even now managing to convey the distance that separated them. He wanted to get the boy into conversation, but could think of nothing to talk about that wouldn't sound wooden and contrived. He knew there must be a common plane of interest somewhere if he only knew what it was. The boy seemed content to walk along in silence, so he retreated into his own thoughts as they entered the business street that led to the church.

As they passed the schoolyard he asked the boy how the softball team was doing.

"All right. We beat the Tigers yesterday."

"What score?"

"Fifteen-eight."

"Say, that's great! Did you score any runs?"

"One, on Jimmy Agnew's two-bagger."

"Great! Did you put many guys out?"

"No."

He realized that he didn't even know what position his own son played, or even the name of the team. He thought it might be the Cardinals, but it might even be the Eskimos. He tried to picture the name on the front of the boy's sweater, but could not recall it.

"How many more games do you play?" he asked.

"Just two more in the regular schedule, one with the Eskimos tomorrow night, and one on Saturday with the Cardinals."

Well, the team wasn't the Tigers, Eskimos or Cardinals. He tried without success to think of the names of the other teams in the league. When they got home he'd have to take a peek at the name on the sweater.

They walked the rest of the way to the church in silence.

A young man in a clerical collar greeted them at the door to the parish hall, introducing himself as Mr. Redpath, the curate.

"My name's John Purcell," he said, smiling and shaking the curate's hand.

"How do you do. Though I know Johnny, and also Mrs. Purcell and your daughter Joanne, this is the first time I've had the pleasure of meeting you I believe."

"Yes it is."

He was a little put out to discover that his family had a life separate from his. Of course they went to church fairly regularly, while he never went at all. When he was asked if he attended church he always answered, "Not since I was marched there with the army."

The young curate didn't seem to know what to do now that they had been introduced. He turned to the boy and asked, "How is the swimming coming along, Johnny?"

"Fine, Mr. Redpath."

The curate said, "He's going to be a great swimmer someday, is your son."

"Yes I know," he answered. Though he was aware that the boy had been going two nights a week to a neighbourhood high school pool, he had never thought of him being an exceptional swimmer. He seemed to know less about the boy than anyone.

They were interrupted by the appearance of the scout-master, a very tall man with glasses, wearing a Boy Scout shirt and long khaki trousers.

Mr. Redpath said, "Mr. Purcell, I'd like you to meet Bob Wooley, the scoutmaster."

"How do you do," he said, putting out his hand. He noticed the two Second World War medal ribbons on the man's left breast, and knew the scoutmaster had never left the country.

The man peered at him as he took his hand. "I'm sorry, I didn't catch the name," he said.

"Purcell," he told him, his smile frozen on his lips.

"Oh yes, Johnny Purcell's father!"

He managed an amiable nod, but decided that the scout-master had come up to expectations.

"Well, Mr. Purcell, I have a disagreeable duty to perform," the man said, pulling a sheaf of tickets from the pocket of his shirt. Holding out two of them he said, "That will be three dollars please," giggling at the curate.

He decided to get into the spirit of the thing, and as he reached for his wallet he said, "Three dollars! Why I could have taken Johnny to a burlesque show for less than that."

The curate and the scoutmaster snickered politely, but he noticed them exchange significant glances. He handed over the money and pocketed the tickets.

"Right upstairs, Mr. Purcell," Redpath said, his tone much cooler than it had been.

When he looked around for the boy he found he had disappeared, and he climbed to the banquet hall alone.

It was a large room, probably used for the Sunday-school. It had an odour of sanctity about it, an almost forgotten smell of hymnbooks and varnish that carried him back to his choir-boy days. Down the middle of the floor stretched two long plank tables supported on sawhorses, and covered with paper tablecloths. There were about fifty places set. Hanging on the walls were various exhibits of scoutcraft, and in one corner of the floor a tent and an imitation campfire had been set up, surrounded by imitation grass probably borrowed from the church cemetery next door.

He spied his son, in the company of two other boys and their fathers, looking at some photographs on the wall, and walked over to them. As soon as he reached his side, Johnny led him away from the others and began pointing out the various knots that were illustrated by twisted pieces of sashcord mounted on a board.

"Have you anything on exhibition, Johnny?" he asked the boy.

"Only the Cree mask I made last winter."

Cree mask! He'd never seen the boy making a mask, though he had wondered vaguely what he was doing in the basement sometimes. "Let's go over and see it," he said, and the boy led him around the tables to the opposite wall.

They stopped before a wooden mask, painted red and yellow with holes cut in it for the eyes and mouth. He was no judge of such things but he was amazed at the workmanship and artistry of it. He could see the tremendous amount of work that had gone into its carving, and felt an immeasurable loss as he realized he had not even enquired what the boy was doing all those long evenings in the basement.

"Say, Johnny, that's great! It's just great!" he said, slapping his son on the shoulder. "I never knew you could make things like that. Did you carve it out of a single piece of wood?"

"No. I had to glue two pieces together."

"Where did you get it — the wood I mean?"

"Mr. Robertson gave me it. He helped me shape it, but I did most of the carving."

"Who's Mr. Robertson?"

"Don's dad. *You* know Don Robertson."

"Oh sure." He didn't know one boy or girl who came to the house from another. It must be the tall blond kid who went to the movies with Johnny on Saturday afternoons.

Two boys and their fathers came along and stood beside them, admiring the mask. He was about to tell them it was the work of his boy, but Johnny was suddenly in a hurry to get away. "Come on, Dad," he said quickly. "There's a picture over here of Danny Mahaffey winning his mountaineer badge."

He followed the boy to the end of the room, aware for the first time that his son was ashamed of him. As he pretended to look at the photograph he wondered what he had ever done to make the boy feel that way. Now he remembered the times he had met Johnny with his friends on the street, and had received only a grudging wave of the hand from him. And he remembered going to watch the boy play ball in the school-yard, and being pointedly ignored throughout the game.

The dinner consisted of the usual creamed chicken and peas, and the after dinner speeches contained the usual intramural jokes shared by the scoutmaster, the curate and the boys. During the meal he became quite friendly with the father sitting on his right, not realizing until it was too late that he had acted over-loquacious, his earlier drinks, plus the heat of the hall, making him talk and laugh too loudly. Once he stopped himself in time before criticizing the scout-master's home service ribbons.

Johnny hardly spoke to him at all, but attached himself conversationally to a boy sitting on the other side of him. They laughed at the speakers' jokes and whispered conspiratorially, ignoring him completely.

From the anecdotes of the speakers he was surprised to find that many of the fathers had visited the summer camp, and that some even joined in the weekend hikes. He had been under the impression that only the scoutmaster and his assistant went along with the boys. He began to feel like an outsider, and he glanced along the line of adult faces across the table, wondering if he was alone in his feelings. Every other father had the look of belonging.

Just when the curate's stories were beginning to gripe him, that young man ended his speech and announced a five-minute break before the presentations would be made. With a loud clattering of chairs the boys and their fathers pushed themselves away from the tables.

When he looked around for Johnny he saw him running towards the stairway in company with the boy who had been sitting beside him. He pushed his way through the crowd to the back door of the hall, and stood on the outside steps and lit a cigarette.

The door behind him opened and a man came out.

"It's kind of stuffy in there," the man said.

"Yes, in more ways than one."

The man laughed. "You said it. This is the first time I ever came to one of these things."

"Me too."

"Good. I was afraid I was the only one."

"My name's Purcell — John Purcell," he said, offering the other his hand.

"Glad to know you, John. I'm Charley Murdoch — Murdoch's Radio and Appliances up on Lorimer Street."

"Sure, I've seen your place."

"What line of business are you in?"

"I'm with Saunders, Gordon and Company, real estate and industrial appraisers."

"Fine."

Murdoch lit a cigarette and they stood talking about the Boy Scouts and their unfamiliarity with dinners such as this one. They discovered they had a couple of mutual friends downtown.

Then Murdoch said, "This may not be the exact place for it, but I've got a bottle of liquor in the car. Would you care for a snort before we go back to hear how the curate got marooned on the island in Elk Lake, or how the scoutmaster's tent blew down in the storm last summer?"

"You're a lifesaver," he said.

They walked to Murdoch's car, which was parked against the cemetery wall. Murdoch took a pint of whiskey from the glove compartment, and then began to feel around in the back seat. "I've got a small bottle of ginger-ale back here somewhere," he said. "Yeah, here she is!" He straightened up and took the top off the ginger-ale with a practised motion beneath the dashboard.

They had three good drinks apiece before Murdoch said, "Maybe we'd better go back inside. If we don't get in there soon that kid of mine will tell his mother for sure."

The presentations were well under way by the time they returned to the hall, and there was a craning of necks by almost everyone as they crossed the floor. As each boy's name was called, he and his father would go forward to the dais, where the scoutmaster presented the badges to the father, who then presented them to his son.

Johnny gave him an apprehensive look when he sat down, and then crowded as far away from him as he could get, trying to associate himself with the boy and his father on the other side of him.

He sat back in his chair and gave his attention to what was taking place on the platform, smiling to himself as the boys and their fathers left the tables, received their presentations, and returned to their seats. As the whiskey began to work he took a friendlier view of the affair, and applauded heartily as each twosome sat down. He mentioned to his neighbour that it looked like an investiture at Buckingham Palace, but the man shushed him with a finger placed to his lips. Once, he tried to catch Murdoch's eye, but his new friend was looking somewhere else.

When the Assistant Scoutmaster called out, "John Purcell," he tapped his son on the shoulder and stood up, saying, "That's both of us." There were a few titters from the boys, and a couple of the fathers smiled. Johnny hurried to the platform without waiting for him. He followed, grinning at the upturned faces he passed. Now that he was on his feet the room began to blur, and the faces at the tables seemed to run together into one big bemused grin. He grinned back, feeling a fellowship with every other father in the room. They really weren't a bad bunch once you got to know them.

As he climbed the steps to the dais the scoutmasters stared at him with a quizzical look, and the curate turned to the audience with an embarrassed smile. The scoutmaster approached him and said, "Mr. Purcell, I am happy and honoured to present this lifesaving certificate to your son, John Purcell, and also this badge for hobbycraft. It is not very often that a boy as young as John earns a lifesaving certificate, and I'm sure you must be very proud of him."

He nodded his head and murmured his thanks. When he looked down to face the boy the room swam before his eyes, but he managed to stay erect. "Here you are, Johnny," he said, handing the boy the certificate and badge. He felt prouder than he had ever felt in his life before, and just handing the awards to his son like this didn't seem enough to mark the moment. In a paroxysm of pride and happiness he grasped the boy's hand, and facing the audience, held it aloft like a referee signifying the winner of a boxing bout.

There was a short burst of embarrassed laughter from the tables. He turned to the scoutmaster, who was trying to smile, with little success. The boy broke away from him and ran back to his chair, his chin lowered on his chest.

He stepped down carefully from the dais, and with all the dignity at his command made his way to his table. As he turned around its end he staggered slightly and fell against it, pushing the planks askew from the saw-horse that supported them. Two or three of the fathers prevented the whole thing from toppling, but a vase of flowers and a couple of plates fell to the floor with a loud crash.

After apologizing profusely to those who were picking up the flowers from the floor, he reached his chair with extra-careful steps and sat down. Some of the small boys stared at him wonderingly, but their fathers showed an absorbing interest in what was going on upon the platform. He now saw the humour of the accident, and turned to wink at his son to show that everything had turned out all right after all. The boy was sobbing silently, his thin shoulders shuddering beneath his blazer.

Suddenly he was shamed by the enormity of his act, and had to prevent himself from taking his son on his knee and comforting him as he had done when the boy was younger. He pulled himself together instead, setting his mouth in a defiant line, and stared unseeing at the people on the platform.

When the meeting came to an end he was the first person out of the hall. He walked about fifty yards down the street and stood in the shadows of the cemetery wall. The boy hurried down the steps and came running towards him, and when he drew abreast he stepped out and took him by the arm.

"I'm sorry, Johnny," he said, placing his arm around the small boy's shoulders. "I acted a little silly in there, but it was really nothing. It'll be forgotten in a day or two."

The boy turned his tear-stained face up to him and said, "Leave me alone, Daddy, please."

"Look, Johnny, I'm sorry. I didn't mean to hurt you like that. Listen, I'll tell you what we'll do — we'll go downtown tomorrow and I'll buy you a whole new Boy Scout outfit."

"I'm not going to the Scouts any more."

"Sure you are. Listen, you've got that lifesaving certificate and —"

"I left them behind. I don't want them any more."

"But Johnny, listen —"

"Leave me alone, Daddy, please!" the boy cried, breaking away from him and running down the street.

"Johnny! Wait for me. Johnny! Listen, I want —"

The boy was half a block away by now, running as fast as he could. He hurried after him, knowing it was useless but afraid to let him go like this. Why had he done it, he asked himself, but could get no answer from either his head or his heart. Had there always been something between himself and the boy that neither of them understood? "No," he said to himself. "No, it's your fault. It's always been your fault."

Already the running form of the boy was two blocks ahead of him, and he would soon be out of sight entirely. As he hurried after him he wondered if he would ever be able to draw close to his son again.

Grandfather's Special Magic

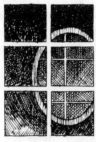

As he ran from the cabin into the early morning sunlight, the slight, copper-coloured boy could see his grandfather in the paddock working with the new pony. Calling and waving his hand, the boy ran to the fence and climbed onto the top rail.

The sudden movement startled the chestnut horse and she reared, thrashing her hooves and straining to be free of the rope looped around her neck. Her thick, golden mane flew as her head tossed angrily from side to side.

For a moment the boy sat motionless, realizing he had forgotten one of Grandfather's first rules for being around a horse — always to move slowly and quietly. With a whinny that echoed shrilly through the still air, the pony slammed her feet to the ground her flashing eyes fixed on the old man. He held firmly to the rope's free end and murmured a steady flow of comforting words in an effort to calm her.

Then the mare raised her head and

ELIZABETH
KAUFMAN

began to pull back. The boy saw Grandfather's powerful arms and legs tense as he braced himself against her strength. The murmurings continued but she paid no attention. Holding her ears flat against her head she had a mean and nasty look.

Suddenly, the pony bared her teeth and struck out. She missed her target, whirled her hindquarters round and, with a vicious kick, lashed out once again.

The old man stood calm and steady. He was used to such behaviour. Each year, between seeding and harvest, he took wild ponies caught in Saskatchewan and brought the long journey by dealers onto his small farm to train. People said he had a special magic to make a horse listen and obey. Sometimes they came from miles around to watch the tall, muscular Indian at work. Now, using his murmurings along with his firm and gentle ways, he had once again begun the game of perseverance: teaching trust to a wild and frightened creature.

Fascinated, the boy watched as the thin little pony galloped in a circle, her hooves thumping over the dry earth and throwing small clouds of dust into the air. He could see that she had begun to sweat and that moisture dampened her hide.

His grandfather raised his voice, giving a single command, "Whoa girl, whoa." With a light tug on the rope the old man repeated the order.

Ignoring him, the pony continued to race wildly. The command was given again until gradually she began to shorten her stride. Finally she moved in an easy trot and the old man spoke words of praise.

The boy on the fence was filled with happiness. Every summer he travelled many miles north to this, the Muskoka region of Ontario. There was joy for him in the journeys for here he could be called by his Indian name, Little Cloud. Back home, in the city, his Indian name was not even known.

He pushed his dark hair from his eyes. It was the summer of his twelfth birthday. More this year than ever before he dreamed of one day having a horse of his own. Perhaps, he thought, Grandfather would even let him train his own pony sometime. That time would be a long way off though. He knew that. The ponies brought in necessary dollars. To give one away would be more than Grandfather could afford.

Already, although her eyes remained watchful, the chestnut pony appeared less frightened. She continued to sweat and Little Cloud could see she was tiring. He was pleased when Grandfather again gave the command, "Whoa," and she dropped to a walk.

"Good girl, good girl," Grandfather said.

Walking in a smaller circle, the pony watched Grandfather out of the corner of her eye her nostrils once again snorting and snuffling in response to his closeness.

"Easy girl, easy now," he murmured.

With a light pressure on the rope he was able to make her come to a halt and stand. Very slowly, he placed the rope end behind his back. At the movement, the pony's eyes flew wide open and she stiffened. Nickerings came from her throat as she raised her head ready to pull back.

Grandfather stood without moving until the pony once more relaxed. Continuing his murmurings, he went silently over the soft earth towards her and stood beside her head. Very gently, he began to blow into one of her nostrils. Her eyes spoke her alarm on feeling his warm breath but when he ceased blowing and resumed his murmurings she stood waiting. Very timidly she moved her face closer to him. Stretching her slender neck until her velvet muzzle touched the side of his cheek she breathed into his nose.

Speaking his gentle words and again breathing into the pony's nostril, Grandfather slowly raised his hand and placed it on the pony's neck. With each calm stroke, his special magic started to work. The boy's heart filled with pride. Slowly, Grandfather began to move and, understanding, the pony began to follow.

Quietly, Little Cloud lowered himself from the fence and walked over to the gate. He joined Grandfather as the old man was praising the little mare and slipping the rope from around her neck.

Free to run, she turned and raced to the far side of the paddock. The boy and his Grandfather stood outside it watching her. She stopped, looking in their direction with obvious curiosity. As they moved away, she suddenly trotted to the fence and whinnied at them. Little Cloud glanced at his Grandfather and smiled.

After breakfast, Little Cloud carried a pail of water over to the paddock, placing it on the hook inside the gate. At the sight of him, the pony snorted and ran in tight circles flattening her ears and tossing her head. He thought she was going to charge at him. Although he was not frightened of horses, he had listened to his Grandfather enough to know he must never trust any animal completely.

Like Grandfather, he began to murmur. The pony's ears pricked up at the sound and she stopped circling to prance about on the spot. She was definitely listening to his soothing words. For a moment he hoped she would come closer but she did not. He left the paddock and joined the old man who was at work in the vegetable garden beside the cabin. All during the morning, the boy listened for the pony's anxious whinnies.

Before bed each evening from then on, Grandfather and Little Cloud went to the paddock to check the pony, paying especial attention to the manger which held her feed. Always the grain remained untouched. This caused Grandfather to worry partly because she was growing thinner and thinner; and partly because, if she did not eat, she could not be expected to work. If she could not be worked she would never be trained. She would have to be returned to the dealer rather than sold.

Little Cloud worried too. Noticing the grass along the fence-line of the paddock was dry and dusty, he decided to gather handfuls of tender green grass from the field beyond the garden and bring it to the pony. She would not eat while he remained in the paddock so he left the grass in a small pile on the ground. When he came back it was completely gone.

After that, he brought grass to the paddock several times each day. Soon the pony began to run over to him. She would come just close enough to make his heart race with excitement and then she would stop. She would stand very still and stare at him with her wide, dark eyes. He would murmur just like his grandfather. Each day she looked more gentle but she would not come any closer.

One day, it occurred to Little Cloud that he should take some grass and mix it with the pony's feed. Perhaps that way she could be tempted to nibble at her grain. He carried out his plan but he was disappointed for when he checked the manger only the grass had disappeared.

Despite Little Cloud's efforts, the chestnut pony grew still thinner. In time, her knees looked knobby and her hips stuck out so far Grandfather said a man could hang his hat on them. Her neck seemed to stretch longer and longer. Her mane became dull and limp, and her tail did not switch so sharply any more. At last, Grandfather said they would have to rest her.

"Could we try her just one more day?" Little Cloud asked. "Please, Grandfather. I would like to help you." Smiling, the old man agreed.

As light began to fill the cabin next morning, a whinny awoke Little Cloud. Throwing back his quilt and pulling on his jeans, he raced outside. He could see Grandfather had already placed the rope around the pony's neck and was waiting for him.

That day, Little Cloud stood close to his Grandfather, turning with him as the old man lunged the pony in a wide circle on a long rope. At the end of the lesson, the boy asked if he could hold the rope while the pony cooled down. Gently, the old man placed it in his hand.

If the pony knew what had happened, she never changed her smooth gait. Proudly, Little Cloud allowed her to circle a few times and then gave the command, "Whoa." A look of surprise followed by a broad smile appeared on his Grandfather's face.

"Whoa," Little Cloud commanded again. A surge of excitement swept through him as he increased the pressure on the pony's neck and began to feel himself gaining control of her. "Whoa," he demanded once more and to his delight she slowed her pace to an easy walk, her dark eyes showing an increased trust of him.

As the pony came to a halt, Little Cloud gathered the rope in his hands and placed it behind his back. He was beginning to move closer, murmuring the familiar sounds, when he felt Grandfather's hand on his shoulder.

"Enough, Little Cloud," Grandfather cautioned. "Do not teach too much too soon or you will undo everything."

The boy nodded to show he understood. He hoped with all his heart that the pony would soon start to eat and grow strong so he could try again.

The next morning, when Little Cloud went out to check the pony's water, he was surprised to find her lying on the ground. Although she was not asleep, she was drowsy. As he moved about the paddock she stayed where she was, watching him with heavy eyes. He knew then that she was sick. He turned and left the paddock, running to tell Grandfather.

Together he and the old man returned. The pony was indeed sick, Grandfather said. She must be left to rest and given plenty to drink. For the next two days, she moved very little and then only to take small sips of water or to seek shade from the large maple tree which protected the end of the paddock from the sun. When she got up, she stood with her head drooping almost to the ground, her ears and tail flicking only occasionally at the flies buzzing round her.

Hour after hour Little Cloud sat watching her. He spoke all the comforting words he knew and at times she would lift her head and gaze sadly at him. Then, on the third day of the pony's illness, as Little Cloud dropped yet more tender grass into her manger she walked toward him. She was still not quite close enough to touch but she had come closer than ever before. He took up a handful of grass and grain and held it out to her on the palm of his hand. She nickered a moment, twisting and wriggling her nose before moving further forward. Edging up, a step at a time, she finally felt his hand and nudged her nose into the feed he offered. The grain flew through the air and onto the ground. With her soft tongue, she picked up the bits of grass.

Now, at last, Little Cloud knew that the pony would come to him; but he knew too that all was useless if she would not eat. Lying awake that night, he prayed for an answer to her problem. In his sleepiness, his prayers bound and wove themselves into the stories Grandfather had told about the past when he had fished and hunted and paddled a canoe; when Grandmother had made adornments from beads and porcupine quills, and baskets from strips of ash wood. They were part too of Grandfather's wisdom and love of the land, his wish always to belong to it, his feeling that rocks and trees and streams had a living presence. Little Cloud could not tell where one thing began and the other ended but in the morning he found he had thought of something he might try.

While Grandfather worked in the far meadow, Little Cloud picked up the rope and headed for the paddock. Placing the loop over the pony's head took longer than he had imagined but in the end he managed it. She seemed to sense that he meant only to help for although she kept her eyes on him she appeared less nervous. With the end of the rope in one hand and his other on her neck he began to lead her around the paddock, murmuring softly all the while. She followed easily. When he felt she trusted him completely he opened the gate so that they could move out through it into the grassy area beyond the garden.

At first as they went the pony skittered about with the rope taut but once she had made a few circles round the boy she began to settle. At the sight of the hayfield, she immediately dropped her head and grazed hungrily. In the midst of her eating though, she would suddenly jerk her head upward and stare out over the countryside. She seemed more alert. Little Cloud could not help feeling that she was better already.

Together they walked on until the pony caught the sounds of water bubbling over the pebbles of a narrow stream bed. The sudden noise startled her. She stiffened and for a moment the boy was afraid she would run. He knew that if she got away they would not likely find her again.

Allowing her to take her time and talking to her he urged her forward. He was pleased to see her interest in the sparkling water. With her neck flexed and her eyes brighter than he had ever seen them she moved nearer and nearer to the stream's bank. Then she seemed to tremble. He reassured her and she lowered her head to take a drink.

It was a happy morning. As the boy and the little chestnut mare wandered away from the stream along a path leading through the woods she grabbed at overhead leaves and pulled at thick clumps of grass. She seemed to be enjoying herself and now there was no doubt in his mind that she was most definitely better. He let his thoughts wander to a time far in the future when he was grown. It was his dearest wish to come back then to the rocky ridges and small farms, the lakes and ravines of Muskoka, to gain his living as his Grandfather did.

The sun moved overhead. Little Cloud remembered that the old man would soon return to the cabin and might be anxious. Whistling softly, he led the way back along the path while the pony followed trustingly behind. He did not take her directly to the paddock, however, but instead went over to the barrel where the feed was kept. Reaching into it, he brought out a handful of grain. This time she at once wriggled her nose deep into the palm of his hand. Soon, he could hear the sound of her teeth grinding the small kernels. He moved his face close to her neck and breathed the warmth of her. He had never felt happier.

In the paddock, the pony stood quietly as Little Cloud removed the rope from her neck. He had just finished when he caught sight of Grandfather walking towards them.

"Grandfather," he called. "Hurry, I have something to tell you."

The old Indian opened the gate and joined them. "You don't have to tell me, Little Cloud, I can see," he said. "It appears, my son, that you also have a special magic."

He placed his arm proudly around his grandson's shoulders. "What name will you give your pony?" he went on.

The boy looked into the pony's large, dark eyes. "I shall call her Little Fawn," he answered. Then, he turned to his grandfather questioningly. "*My* pony? Did you say *my* pony, Grandfather?" he asked.

The old man answered with his gentle, broad smile.

"My very own pony! I can't believe it!" The boy wanted to jump high into the air and to yell the news to all of Muskoka. But, he remembered Grandfather's rule — move slowly and quietly. Instead he put out his hand and let Little Fawn nuzzle her nose into it. He could jump and yell later.

Lark Song

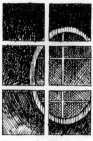

If we'd of been smart we never would have let Joseph go off by himself that Saturday in Wetaskiwin. But we did, and there sure been a lot of trouble for everybody ever since. My brother, Joseph Ermineskin, be older than me. He is 22 already, but when he just a baby he catch the scarlet fever and his mind it never grow up like his body do.

Joseph ain't crazy. He just got a tiny kid's mind in a big man's body. He is close to six feet tall and broad across the shoulder. His face is round and the colour of varnished wood. He be gentle and never hurt nobody in his whole life.

Unless you look right in his eyes he don't look no different than the rest of us guys. We let his hair grow long, and we got him a denim outfit, and once when I worked at a mine for the summer, I bought him a pair of cowboy boots. But Joseph he smile too often and too long at a time. I guess it because his mind ain't full of worries like everybody else.

Joseph ain't no more trouble to look after than any other little kid and he is even good at a couple of things. He can hear a song on the radio and then play it

W. P. KINSELLA

back on my old guitar just like he heard it. He forget it pretty quick though, and can usually only do it one time.

And he can sound like birds. He caws like the crows so good that they come to see where the crow is that's talking to them. He talk like a magpie too, but best of all he sound like a meadowlark. Meadowlarks make the prettiest sound of any bird I ever heard, when they sing it sound like sweet water come bubble up out of a spring.

Sometime when we sit around the cabin at night and everyone is sad, Joseph he make that lark song for us and soon everyone is feel some better because it so pretty.

It is funny that he can do that sound so good, cause when he talk he sound like the wind-up record player when it not cranked up good enough. His voice is all slow and funny and he have to stop a long time between words.

One time, Papa, when he still lived here with us, is take Joseph with him to Wetaskiwin. Papa he get drunk and don't come home for a week or so, but the very next day, Joseph he is show up. He is hungry and tired from walk all those miles down the highway, but he find his way home real good. He is smile clear around to the back of his neck when he see us, and he don't ask about go to town with anybody for a long time after that.

Still I can tell he feel bad when me and my friend Frank Fence-post and all the guys go into town in Louis Coyote's pickup truck and leave him at home. That was why we take him one Saturday afternoon with us. We put him in the park to play while we go look in the stores and maybe stop for a beer or two. Joseph sure like the swings, and being strong and tall he can sure swing up high. What we should of told him though, and didn't, was for sure not to play with none of them white kids.

White people don't like nobody else to touch their kids, especially Indians. Here on the reserve it's kind of like one family, the kids run free when they is little and nobody minds if somebody else hugs your little boy or girl.

Joseph he like little kids and they like him back. Big people don't always have time, or maybe they don't want to, love their kids as much as they should. Joseph is pick up the kids when they fall down, or maybe when they is just lonesome. He don't say nothing to them, just pet their heads like maybe they was little kittens, hold them close and make them feel warm. Sometimes he make his bird sounds for them, and they forget why they feel bad, hug his neck, and feel good that someone likes them.

People say that was what happen in the park in Wetaskiwin that day. A little white girl is fall off the slide and hurt herself. When Joseph see her crying he is just pick her up like he would an Indian kid. Only them kids all been told, don't mess around with strangers, and somebody runs for some mothers.

We come back to get Joseph about the same time that little girl's mother come to get her. If you ever seen a lady partridge fly around on the ground pretend she got a broken wing so her enemy go after her and leave her young ones alone, that is how that white lady is act.

Joseph is just stand in the sandbox hold that little girl in his arms, and she is not even crying anymore until she hear her mother scream and dance up and down. I sure afraid for what might have happen to Joseph if we don't come when we did.

I unwrap his arms from the little girl and hand her back to the lady, who is cry some and yell a lot of bad things at us and say somebody already called the RCMP.

The RCMP guys come roll up in their car with the lights flash and I sure wish we was all someplace else. While everyone try to yell louder than everyone else, Joseph he sit down and play some in the sand and every once in a while he is make his meadowlark call.

I try to explain to them RCMP guys that Joseph he is about as harmless as that meadowlark he is sounding like. Meadowlarks ain't very pretty or good for much but make beautiful sounds, but they sure don't hurt nobody either, I tell them.

Lots of people is standing around watching and I think they

figure something real bad has happened. There is a real big white lady with a square face is carry a shotgun.

We promise the RCMP guys and anybody else that will listen that for sure we never gonna bring Joseph to town no more. We keep him on the reserve forever and then some, we tell them.

For once it look like maybe the RCMP is gonna believe us Indians. They say they can't see no reason to lay any charges, cause all it look like Joseph done was to pick up a kid that fall down. The white girl's mother is yell loud on everybody, say if the RCMP ain't gonna do nothing she'll go to somebody who will. And that lady with the square face wave her shotgun and say she would sure like to shoot herself a few wagon-burners.

After we all go to the police station for a while the RCMP guys let us take Joseph home, but it is only a couple of days until some Government people is come nose around our place a lot. They is kind of like the coyotes come pick at the garbage, we hardly ever see them but we still know they is there.

Two little women in brown suits come to our cabin, say wouldn't we think Joseph be happier in a home someplace where there are lots of other retarded guys.

Ma, like she always do, pretend she don't understand English, and just sit and look at them with a stone face. But she sure is worried.

Next time they come back, they ain't nearly so nice. They say either we put Joseph in the place for crazy people at Ponoka, or they get a judge to tell us we have to.

The next week, me and my girlfriend Sadie One-wound, hitch-hike the twelve miles down to Ponoka to have a look at the crazy place. I know all my life that the place is there but there is something about a place like that that scares us a lot. It make us too shy to go up to the gate and ask to look around. Instead we just walk around outside for a while. It got big high wire fences but inside there is lots of grass and beds of pretty flowers, and the people who walk around inside don't look as though they trying to run away or nothing.

The Government peoples keep sending Ma big fat letters with red writing on them. One say that Ma and Joseph got to appear at something called a committal hearing at the court room in Wetaskiwin. We figure that if we go there they gonna take Joseph away from us for sure.

I go down to the pay phone at Hobbema Crossing and phone all the way to Calgary to the office of Mr. William Wuttunee, the Indian lawyer, but he is away on holiday, and no, I say, I don't want nobody to call me or nothing.

We don't go to that committal hearing cause Ma, she say that we just pretend that nothing is happening, and if we do that long enough the white people stop bothering us.

A couple of weeks later we get another big bunch of papers with red seals all over them, delivered by the RCMP guys personal. Them papers say they gonna come and get Joseph on a certain date. We figure it out on the calendar from the Texaco Service Station, and we decide that when they come they ain't gonna find no Joseph. We just put him to live with someone back in the bush a few miles and move him around whenever we have to.

One good thing about white people is that they usually give up easy. The RCMP is always nose around for Sam Standing-at-the-door's still, or maybe have a warrant for arrest somebody for steal car parts or something, but we tear up the culvert in the road from Hobbema to our cabins, and them guys sure hate to walk much, so they just go away after they yell at the closest Indians for a while. We figure the Government people like to walk even less than the RCMP so it be pretty easy to fool them.

I don't know if they came a day early or if maybe we forget a day someplace, but their cars is already across the culvert and halfway up the hill before we see them. And the guy from the crazy place in Ponoka, who wears a white jacket, look like he be a cook in a café, say he is a Métis, and he even talk Cree to us, which is real bad, cause then we can't pretend we don't understand what is happening. Usually, people we don't like go away real quick when we pretend we don't understand, especially if we sharpen a knife or play with a gun while we talk about them some in our language.

This Métis guy tell us, look, they ain't gonna hurt Joseph down there at the mental hospital, and it only be twelve miles away so we can come visit him anytime. He gonna be warm and clean and have lots of food and he get to make friends with other guys like him and maybe even learn to make things with his hands and stuff.

It don't sound so bad after all, if it true what he says. All we had time to do was hide Joseph under the big bed in the cabin, and he been making bird songs all the time he is under there. Ma, she finally call him to come out, and he poke out his head and smile on everybody.

We pack up his clothes in a cardboard box. He sure ain't got much to take with him. Frank Fence-post ask them guys if they got electric light down at the crazy place, and they tell him the hospital is fully equipped. Frank he goes and gets his fancy-shaped electric guitar that he bought at a pawnshop in Calgary. He tell the guys from the hospital they should show Joseph how to plug the guitar into the wall. Then he shove the guitar into Joseph's arms.

The kids is all come out from the cabins and stand around look shy at the ground while I talk to Joseph, like I would my littlest sister, explain he should be good, and how these guys is his friends and all. Joseph he pet the guitar like it alive and smile for everybody and touch his fingers on the shiny paint of the car from Ponoka.

Once they is gone we sure ain't got much to say to each other. Me and Frank talk a little about how we go visit Joseph on Saturday, sneak him away and hide him out on the reserve. But it different when they got him than when we got him, and I don't think that idea ever gonna come to much.

I don't sleep so good that night. I am up early. The sky is clear and the sun is just come up. There is frost on the brown grasses and the slough at the foot of the hill is frozen thin as if window glass had been laid across it. Brown bulrushes tipped with frost, stand, some straight, some at angles, like spears been stuck in the ground. Outside the cabin door our dogs lie curled like horse collars in their dirt nests. They half open their yellow eyes, look at me then go to sleep again. The air is thin and clear and pine smoke from another cabin is rise straight up like ink lines on paper. From the woodpile I carry up an armful of split pine. The wood is cold on my arm and I tuck the last piece under my chin.

Then there is like an explosion from down the hill and across the slough someplace. Like a gun shot, only beautiful. The crows rise up like they been tossed out of the spruce trees.

At first I want to laugh it sound so funny, the voice of a summer bird on a frosty morning. Then it come again, that sweet, bubbly, blue-sky-coloured lark song. I do laugh then, but for happy, and I toss the wood on the ground and run for the meadow.

The Woman and the Wolf

The people built the little snowhouse and departed into the western lands. They went from the place singing laments for the dying, and they left nothing behind them except the old man. They took Arnuk, the dog, that being the old man's wish, for Arnuk was the last gift an old man could make to his son and to his grandson and to his people.

It had been a hard time — those long, hungry months before the spring — and in the camp there had been the cries of children who were too young to know that starvation must be faced in silence. There had been death in the camp, not of men but of those who were of the utmost importance to the continuance of human life. The dogs had died, one by one, and as each was stilled so men's hopes for the future shrank.

Though it had been a harsh time, no word had been spoken against the folly of feeding one old and useless human body. Maktuk, the son, had shared his own meagre rations equally between his

FARLEY
MOWAT

aged father and his hungry child who also bore the name that linked the three together. But one dark April day the old man raised himself slowly from the sleeping ledge and gazed for a little while at his grandchild. Then out of the depths of a great love, and a greater courage, old Maktuk spoke:

"I have it in my heart," he said, "that the deer await you at the Western Lakes, but I stay here. You shall take Arnuk with you so that in the years ahead you will remember me."

The old man had his rights, and this was his final one. In the morning the people were gone, and behind young Maktuk's sled the dog Arnuk tugged convulsively at her tether and turned her head backward to stare at a small white mound rising against the snow ridges.

Arnuk had been born two winters earlier, but she was the ninth pup of the litter and so there was little food for her. If the old man had not taken it upon himself to feed and care for her, she would have died before her life truly began. With his help she saw warm days come and tasted the pleasures of long days romping with other young dogs by the side of the great river where the summer camp was pitched. When she grew tired she would come to the skin tent and push against the old man's knees until he opened his eyes and smiled at her.

So she grew through the good times of youth and the people in the camp looked at her with admiration for she became beautiful and of a size and strength surpassing that of any other dog in the camp. Maktuk, the elder, gave her the name she bore, Arnuk — The Woman — for she was wife and daughter to him in the autumn of his years.

Because there can be no death while there is birth, old Maktuk decided in mid-winter that his dog should be mated, although famine had already struck the camp. It was arranged, and so Arnuk bore within her the promise of a strength which would be the people's strength in years to come. When Maktuk, the elder, felt the throb of new life in the womb of The Woman, he was content.

Hunger grew with the passing days. The older dogs died

first, then even Arnuk's litter mates lay silent in the snows. But Arnuk's strength was great; and when there was some scrap of bone or skin the people could spare, she received it — for in her womb lay the hopes of years to come.

This was the way things stood when the people turned from the little snowhouse and set their faces to the west, dragging the sleds with their own failing muscles.

The ties that bind man and his dog can be of many strengths, but the ties that bound Arnuk to old Maktuk were beyond human power to sunder. Arnuk went with the people, but resisting stubbornly. On the third night of the journey she gnawed through the rawhide tether and vanished into the swirling ground drift. In the morning Maktuk, the son, held the frayed tether in his hand and his face was shadowed by foreboding. Yet when he spoke to his family it was with these words:

"The Woman has gone to my father and she will be with him when the Snow Walker comes. But my father's spirit will know of our need, and perhaps the day will dawn when he will return The Woman to us."

Arnuk reached the little igloo before daybreak and when the old man opened his eyes to see if it was the Snow Walker, he saw the dog instead. He smiled and laid his bony hand upon her head, and once more he slept.

The Snow Walker was late in coming, but on the third day he came unseen; and when he passed from the place, the bond between man and dog was broken. Yet Arnuk lingered beside her dead for another day, and then it was perhaps the wind that whispered the unspoken order: "Go to the people. Go!"

When she emerged from the snowhouse she found the plains newly scoured by a blizzard. For awhile she stood in the pale winter sun, her lambent coat gleaming against the blue shadows, then she turned her face with its broad ruff and wide-spaced amber eyes toward the west. That way lay her path, and within her the voices of the unborn generations echoed the voice of the wind but with greater urgency. "Go to the places of men," they told her. "Go!"

Head down and great plume held low, she moved westward into the pathless spaces and only once did she pause to turn and stare at her back trail, waiting for some final sign. There was no sign, and at length she turned away.

This was the beginning of her journey. Death had released her from the ties that held her to one man, but she was still bound fast to Man. Through untold generations stretching back through the long dim sweep of time before the Eskimos drifted east across the island chain from Asia, the fate of her kind had been one with that of Man. Arnuk was one with the people and her need of them was as great as their need of her.

She did not halt when darkness swept the bleak plains into obscurity. At midnight she came to the place where she had chewed her way free of young Maktuk's sled. She knew it was the place only by an inner sense, for the snow had levelled all signs and drifted in all trails. Uncertainty began to feed upon her as she circled among the hard drifts, whining miserably. She climbed a rock ridge to test the night air for some sign that men were near. A scent came to her — the odour of an arctic hare that had fled at her approach. But there was no scent of man.

Her whines rose to a crescendo, pleading in the darkness, but there was no answer except the rising mutter of the wind. Unable to endure the weight of her hunger and loneliness, she curled up in the shelter of a drift and lost herself in dreams.

So the dog slept in the heart of the great plains. But even as she dozed restlessly, a profound change was taking place in the secret places of her body. She lay with her nose outstretched on her broad forepaws and her muscles twitched with erratic impulses. Saliva flowed in her mouth and had the taste of blood. In her mind's eye she laid her stride to that of the swift deer, and her teeth met in the living flesh and she knew the ecstasy of the hunter.

From out of time and ageless instincts which lie in all living cells were being revitalized so that the dog, and the new life within her, would not perish. When Arnuk raised her head to the dawn light, the thing was done, the change complete.

The dawn was clear, and Arnuk, her perceptions newly honed, tested the wind. When she found the warm aroma of living flesh she went to seek it out.

A Snowy Owl, dead white and shadowless in the pre-dawn, had swept across the plains with great eyes staring. The owl had seen and fallen on a hare so swiftly that the beast had known nothing until the inch-long talons took life from him. For a little time the great bird chose to savour its hunger; and while it sat complacently crouched above the hare, it did not see the flow of motion behind a nearby drift.

Arnuk was a weasel easing up on a lemming, a fox drifting toward a ptarmigan. Skills she had never fully known had come alive within her. She inched forward soundlessly over the hard snows. When she was still a few yards from the owl, it raised its head and the yellow eyes stared with expressionless intensity full into Arnuk's face. Arnuk was the stillness of death, yet every muscle vibrated. When the owl turned back to its prey, Arnuk leapt. The owl saw the beginning of the leap and threw itself backward into its own element with a smooth thrust of mighty wings. Those wings were a fraction slow and the hurtling form of the dog, leaping six feet into the air, struck flesh beneath the feathers.

Arnuk slept afterwards while white feathers blew into the distance and tufts of white fur moved like furtive living things in the grip of the wind. When she woke again the age-old voices within her had quieted. Once more she was man's beast, and so she set out again into the west, unconscious yet directly driven.

The people whom she sought were wanderers on the face of a plain so vast that it seemed limitless. The dog could not envisage the odds against her finding them, but in her memory was the image of the summer camp by the wide river where she had spent her youth. She set her mind upon that distant place.

The days passed and the sun stood a little higher in the sky after each one faded. Time passed under the dog's feet until the explosion of spring overwhelmed the tundra. The snows melted and the rivers awoke and thundered seaward. Flights of ravens hung like eddies of burned leaves in a white and glaring sky, and on the thawing ponds the first ducks mingled with raucous flocks of gulls.

Life quickened in the deep moss where the lemmings tunnelled and on the stony ridges where cock ptarmigan postured before their mates. It was in all living things and in all places, and it was within the womb of the dog. Her journey had been long and her broad paws were crusted with the dried blood of many stone cuts. Her coat was matted and lustreless under the spring suns. Still she drew upon her indomitable will and went forward into the western plains.

Gaunt and hot eyed she brought her quest to an end on a day in June. Breasting a long ridge she saw before her the glittering light of sun on roaring water and she recognized the river.

Whining with excitement she ran clumsily down the slope, for her body had grown awkward in these last days. Soon she was among the rings of weathered boulders where, in other summers, men's tents had stood.

No tents stood there now. There were no living men to welcome the return of the lost one. Only the motionless piles of rocks on nearby ridges, that are called *Inukok*, Men of Stone, were there to welcome Arnuk. She understood that the place was abandoned yet for a time she refused to believe it. She ran from old tent ring to old meat cache, sniffing each with a despairing hope, and finding nothing to give her heart. It was dusk before she curled herself in a hollow beside the place where Maktuk, the elder, had once held her at his knees, and gave herself up to her great weariness.

Yet the place was not as deserted as it looked. While Arnuk was making her fruitless search she was too preoccupied to realize that she was being watched. If she had glanced along the river bank she might have seen a lithe shape that followed her every move with eyes that held in them a hunger not born of the belly. She would have seen and recognized a wolf, and her hackles would have risen and her teeth been bared. For the dogs of men and the dogs of the wilderness walk apart, theirs being the hostility of brothers who deny their common blood.

The wolf was young. Born the preceding season, he had stayed with his family until, in the early spring of this year, the urge to wander had come over him and he had forsaken his clan's territory. Many adventures had befallen him and he had learned, at the cost of torn flanks and bleeding shoulders, that each wolf family guards its own land and there is no welcome for a stranger. His tentative approaches had been met with bared teeth in the lands of three wolf clans before he came to the river and found a place where no wolves were.

It was a good place. Not far from the empty Innuit camp the river flared over a shallow stretch of jagged boulders to lose itself in the beginning of an immense lake, and here for centuries the caribou had forded the shallows during their migrations. Two or three times a year they crossed the river in untold thousands, and not all escaped the river's surge. Drowned bodies of dead deer lay among the rocks at the river mouth, giving food to many foxes, ravens and white gulls. The wolves of the country did not visit the place because it belonged to man, and that which man claims to himself is abhorrent to the great wild dogs.

Knowing nothing of this tabu, the young male wolf, the wanderer, had taken up his home by the river; and here he nursed his loneliness, for even more than dogs, wolves are social beings.

When the young wolf saw and smelled Arnuk, he was filled with conflicting emotions. He had seen no dog before but he sensed that the golden-coated beast below him was somehow of his blood. The smell was strange, and yet it was familiar. The shape and colour were strange, and yet they roused in him a warmth of memory and desire. But he had been rebuffed so many times that he was cautious now.

When Arnuk woke she did not at first see the stranger, but her nostrils told her of the nearness of deer meat. Her hunger was overpowering. She leapt to her feet and flung herself upon a ragged haunch of caribou that had been dragged to within a few yards of her sleeping place. Only when she had satisfied her first hunger did she glance up . . . to meet the still gaze of the young wolf.

He sat motionless a hundred feet from her and did not even twitch an ear as Arnuk's hackles lifted and the threat took form deep in her throat. He remained sitting quietly but tense to spring away, and after a long minute Arnuk again dropped her head to the meat.

This was the way of their first meeting, and this is what came of it.

Arnuk could no longer resist the insistent demands of her heavy body. Once again the hidden force within her took command. Ignoring the young wolf, who still cautiously kept his distance, Arnuk made a tour of the familiar ground beside the river. She carefully examined the carcasses of five drowned deer and chased away the screaming gulls and guttural ravens, for this meat was hers now by right of greater strength. Then, satisfied with the abundant food supply, she left the river and trotted inland to where a rock outcrop had opened its flanks to form a shallow cave. Here, as a pup, Arnuk had played with the other dogs of the camp. Now she examined the cave with more serious intent. The place was dry and protected from the winds. There was only one thing wrong, and that was the smell. The rock cleft was pervaded with a potent and unpleasant stench that caused Arnuk to draw back her lips in anger and distaste — a wolverine had bedded in the cave during the winter months.

Arnuk's nose told her that the wolverine had been gone for several weeks, and there seemed little likelihood that he would return until the winter gales again forced him to seek shelter. She scratched earth and sand over the unclean floor, then set about dragging moss into the deepest recess. Here she hid herself and made surrender to her hour.

Arnuk's pups were born on a morning when the cries of the white geese were loud in the spring air. It was the time of birth, and the seven squirming things that lay warm against the dog's fur were not alone in their first day of life. On the sand ridges beyond the river, female ground squirrels suckled naked motes of flesh; and in a den by a ridge a mile distant, an arctic fox thrust his alert face above the ground while the feeble whimpers of the pups his mate was nursing warned him of the tasks ahead. All living things in the land by the river moved to the rhythm of the demands of life newborn or soon to be born. All things moved to this rhythm except the outcast wolf.

During the time Arnuk remained hidden, the young wolf underwent a torment that gave him no peace. Restless and yearning for things he had never known, he haunted the vicinity of the cave. He did not dare go too close, but each day he carried a piece of deer meat to within a few yards of the cave mouth and then drew back to wait hopefully for his gift to be accepted.

On the third day, as he lay near the cave snapping at the flies which hung in a cloud about his head, his keen ears felt the faintest tremors of a new sound. He was on his feet instantly, head thrust out and body tense with attention. It came again, so faint it was felt rather than heard — a tiny whimper that called to him across the ages and across all barriers. He shook himself abruptly and with one quick, proprietary glance at the cave mouth, he trotted out across the plain — no longer a solitary outcast but a male beginning the evening hunt that would feed his mate and pups. So, simply and out of his deep need, the young wolf filled the void that had surrounded him through the torturing weeks of spring.

Arnuk did not so easily accept the wolf in his newly assumed role. For several days she kept him at a distance with bared teeth, although she ate the food he left at the cave mouth. But before a week was out she had come to expect the fresh meat — the tender ground squirrels, arctic hares and plump ptarmigan. From this acceptance it was not a very long step to complete acceptance of the wolf himself.

Arnuk sealed the compact with him during the second week after the pups were born, when, coming to the den mouth one morning, she found part of a freshly killed caribou fawn lying ready for her, and the sleeping form of the young wolf only a few feet away.

The wolf had made a long, hard hunt that night, covering most of the hundred square miles of territory he had staked out for his adopted family. Exhausted by his efforts, he had not bothered to retire the usual discreet distance from the den.

For a long minute Arnuk stared at the sleeping wolf and then she began to stalk him. There was no menace in her attitude and when she reached the wolf's side her great plumed tail went up into its husky curl and her lips lifted as if in laughter.

The wolf woke, raised his head, saw her standing over him and knew that here at last was the end to loneliness. The morning light blazed over the den ridge as the two stood shoulder to shoulder looking out over the awakening plains.

Life was good by the banks of the river during the days that followed. There was no emptiness now in Arnuk's heart. And for the wolf there was the swelling pride with which he lay in the sun outside the den while the pups tussled with his fur and chewed at his feet.

Time passed until the pups were in their seventh week. Midsummer had come to the barrens and the herds of deer were drifting southward again. The crossing place was once more thronged and calves grunted beside their ragged mothers while old bucks, their velvet-covered antlers reaching to the skies, moved aloofly in the van.

One evening a hunger for the chase came over Arnuk, and in the secret ways men know nothing of, she made her desire known to the wolf. When the late summer dusk fell, Arnuk went out alone into the darkening plains, secure in the knowledge that the wolf would steadfastly guard the pups until she returned.

She did not intend a long absence, but several miles from

the river she came on a band of young buck deer. They were fine beasts, and fat, which at this time of the year was unusual. Arnuk was tired of lean meat and she circled the resting herd, filled with an ardent appetite.

A change of the uncertain breeze betrayed her and the startled deer sprang to their feet and fled. Arnuk was hungry and the night was a hunter's night. She took up the long chase.

The hours drove the brief darkness from the land and when the early winds of dawn rose in the north the young wolf roused himself from his vigil at the cave mouth. An ill-defined uneasiness made him turn to the den and thrust his head and shoulders into the entrance. All was well, and the pups were rolled together in a compact ball, jerking their sturdy legs in sleep. Yet the prickle of anxiety persisted in the wolf's mind and he turned toward the river where the grey light picked out the long rolls of distant ridges.

Perhaps he was worried by Arnuk's long absence; or perhaps he had been disturbed by senses unknown to man. He trotted away from the den sniffing at the cold trail of the dog, hoping to see her approaching across the lightening plains.

He had gone no more than a quarter of a mile when the vague sense of something amiss took concrete form. A vagrant eddy brought the north breeze to his nostrils and instantly he knew what had disturbed him when he woke. He sprinted back toward the cave with startling speed.

As he breasted the slope beside the den the stink of wolverine filled his nostrils and he was transformed by an elemental fury. He came down the slope in half a dozen gigantic leaps, ears flat to his skull and his throat rumbling with incoherent rage.

The wolverine which had wintered in the cave where Arnuk's pups now whimpered in their sleep was a sixty-pound male, a little past his prime, and more than a little short of temper. That spring he had methodically searched for a mate across

hundreds of miles of the surrounding country and had found
none. During the night of Arnuk's hunt he had returned to
the ford by the river where he expected to find a good store of
drowned deer. Instead he had found nothing but clean bones
and the evidence that a wolf and a dog had pre-empted what
he considered to be his private larder. His mood grew worse,
and when his wrinkling nostrils caught the faintest trace of
pup smell from the direction of the old winter lair, he did not
hesitate. His belly rumbling with hunger he turned from the
river in the grey dawn light and circled upwind until he found
a rock outcrop that gave him cover and from which he could
observe the den. Here he waited until he saw the young wolf
trot away from the den mouth toward the inland plains.

Cautiously the wolverine moved in upon the den, pausing
to reassure himself that the pups were undefended. His
massive body hugged the rough ground as he drew closer and
now, certain of success, he could foretaste the pleasure of the
killing and the salt warmth of blood.

There was blood enough for him to taste that dawn.

The young wolf's furious rush was so swift that the
wolverine had only time to slew about and take the weight of
the attack upon his side. It was enough to save him for the
moment. Although the wolf's teeth sank into the tough skin,
they missed their intended hold upon the throat, meeting
instead in the muscles of the wolverine's shoulder. On any
lesser beast it would have been a good hold, but on this beast it
was not good enough. Aflame with an incandescent anger, he
swung the wolf clean off its feet as he whirled in a savage
counter-thrust.

Had the wolf been older and more experienced he might
have released his grip and sidestepped that lunge, but he was
young and blinded by the allegiance he had so freely given to
the pups he had not sired. He held his grip and did not slacken
it even when the wolverine's teeth and claws raked deep into
his flank.

They fought in silence. On the eastern rim of the horizon
the red sun seemed pallid beside the glare of blood upon the

rocks. Drawn to the cave mouth by the first onslaught, the pups watched for an instant and then, terrified by the fury of the struggle, retreated to crouch trembling in the dark earth. Only the gulls witnessed the duel's end.

The gulls warned Arnuk. As she trotted wearily homeward in the warmth of the morning, she saw them circling and heard their strident screams. They eddied ominously above the rocks where the den lay and, weary as she was, anxiety gave her new strength and she came on at a gallop. And so she found them. The wolverine had dragged himself toward the river before he bled to death. But the wolf, his belly ripped raggedly so that his entrails sprawled around him, lay stiffening beside the entrance to the cave.

The bodies still lay where they had died when, a few days later, the voices of men echoed once more along the shores of the river, and young Maktuk bent down to the dark opening and gently thrust his hand under the timid pups while Arnuk, half wild with old emotions, stood trembling by his side. Maktuk was a man who could read much that is never written and he understood all there was to know of what had taken place beneath those shattered rocks.

On an evening in late summer he took his son to the bank of the river and placed the boy's hand on the head of the saffron-coated dog.

"Maktuk, my son, in a little time you also shall be a man and a hunter, and the wide plains will know your name. In those days to come you will have certain friends to help you in the hunt, and of these the foremost you shall always call *Arnuk*; and then my father will know that we received his gift and he will be at ease. And in those times to come, all beasts shall fall to your spear and bow, save one alone. Never shall your hand be raised against the white one — against *Amow*, the wolf — and so shall our people pay their debt to him."

Boys and Girls

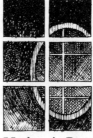

My father was a fox farmer. That is, he raised silver foxes, in pens; and in the fall and early winter, when their fur was prime, he killed them and skinned them and sold their pelts to the Hudson's Bay Company or the Montreal Fur Traders. These companies supplied us with heroic calendars to hang, one on each side of the kitchen door. Against a background of cold blue sky and black pine forests and treacherous northern rivers, plumed adventurers planted the flags of England or of France; magnificent savages bent their backs to the portage.

For several weeks before Christmas, my father worked after supper in the cellar of our house. The cellar was whitewashed, and lit by a hundred-watt bulb over the worktable. My brother Laird and I sat on the top step and watched. My father removed the pelt inside-out from the body of the fox, which looked surprisingly small, mean and rat-like, deprived of its arrogant weight of fur. The naked, slippery bodies were collected in a sack and buried at the dump. One time the hired man, Henry Bailey, had taken a

ALICE
MUNRO

swipe at me with this sack, saying, "Christmas present!" My mother thought that was not funny. In fact she disliked the whole pelting operation — that was what the killing, skinning, and preparation of the furs was called —and wished it did not have to take place in the house. There was the smell. After the pelt had been stretched inside-out on a long board my father scraped away delicately, removing the little clotted webs of blood vessels, the bubbles of fat; the smell of blood and animal fat, with the strong primitive odour of the fox itself, penetrated all parts of the house. I found it reassuringly seasonal, like the smell of oranges and pine needles.

Henry Bailey suffered from bronchial troubles. He would cough and cough until his narrow face turned scarlet, and his light blue, derisive eyes filled up with tears; then he took the lid off the stove, and, standing well back, shot out a great clot of phlegm — hsss — straight into the heart of the flames. We admired him for this performance and for his ability to make his stomach growl at will, and for his laughter, which was full of high whistlings and gurglings and involved the whole faulty machinery of his chest. It was sometimes hard to tell what he was laughing at, and always possible that it might be us.

After we had been sent to bed we could still smell fox and still hear Henry's laugh, but these things, reminders of the warm, safe, brightly lit downstairs world, seemed lost and diminished, floating on the stale cold air upstairs. We were afraid at night in the winter. We were not afraid of *outside* though this was the time of year when snowdrifts curled around our house like sleeping whales and the wind harassed us all night, coming up from the buried fields, the frozen swamp, with its old bugbear chorus of threats and misery. We were afraid of *inside*, the room where we slept. At this time the upstairs of our house was not finished. A brick chimney went up one wall. In the middle of the floor was a square hole, with a wooden railing around it; that was where the stairs came up. On the other side of the stairwell were the things that nobody had any use for any more — a soldiery roll of linoleum, standing on end, a wicker baby carriage, a fern basket, china jugs and basins with cracks in them, a picture of the Battle of Balaclava, very sad to look at. I had told Laird, as soon as he was old enough to understand such things, that bats and skeletons lived over there; whenever a man escaped from the county jail, twenty miles away, I imagined that he had somehow let himself in the window and was hiding behind the linoleum. But we had rules to keep us safe. When the light was on, we were safe as long as we did not step off the square of worn carpet which defined our bedroom-space; when the light was off no place was safe but the beds themselves. I had to turn out the light kneeling on the end of my bed, and stretching as far as I could to reach the cord.

In the dark we lay on our beds, our narrow life rafts, and fixed our eyes on the faint light coming up the stairwell, and sang songs. Laird sang "Jingle Bells," which he would sing any time, whether it was Christmas or not, and I sang "Danny Boy." I loved the sound of my own voice, frail and supplicating, rising in the dark. We could make out the tall frosted shapes of the windows now, gloomy and white. When I came to the part, *When I am dead, as dead I well may be* — a fit of shivering caused not by the cold sheets but by pleasurable emotion almost silenced me. *You'll kneel and say, an Ave there above me* — What was an Ave? Every day I forgot to find out.

Laird went straight from singing to sleep. I could hear his long, satisfied, bubbly breaths. Now for the time that remained to me, the most perfectly private and perhaps the best time of the whole day, I arranged myself tightly under the covers and went on with one of the stories I was telling myself from night to night. These stories were about myself, when I had grown a little older; they took place in a world that was recognizably mine, yet one that presented opportunities for courage, boldness and self-sacrifice, as mine never did. I rescued people from a bombed building (it discouraged me that the real war had gone on so far away from Jubilee). I shot two rabid wolves who were menacing the schoolyard (the teachers cowered terrified at my back). I rode a fine horse spiritedly down the main street of Jubilee, acknowledging the townspeople's gratitude for some yet-to-be-worked-out piece of heroism (nobody ever rode a horse there, except King Billy in the Orangemen's Day parade). There was always riding and shooting in these stories, though I had only been on a horse twice — bareback because we did not own a saddle — and the second time I had slid right around and dropped under the horse's feet; it had stepped placidly over me. I really was learning to shoot, but I could not hit anything yet, not even tin cans on fence posts.

Alive, the foxes inhabited a world my father made for them. It was surrounded by a high guard fence, like a medieval town, with a gate that was padlocked at night. Along the streets of this town were ranged large, sturdy pens. Each of them had a real door that a man could go through, a wooden ramp along the wire, for the foxes to run up and down on, and a kennel — something like a clothes chest with airholes — where they slept and stayed in winter and had their young. There were feeding and watering dishes attached to the wire in such a way that they could be emptied and cleaned from the outside. The dishes were made of old tin cans, and the ramps and kennels of odds and ends of old lumber. Everything was tidy and ingenious; my father was tirelessly inventive and his favourite book in the world was Robinson Crusoe. He had fitted a tin drum on a wheelbarrow, for bringing water down to the pens. This was my job in summer, when the foxes had to have water twice a day. Between nine and ten o'clock in the morning, and again after supper, I filled the drum at the pump and trundled it down through the barnyard to the pens, where I parked it, and filled my watering can and went along the streets. Laird came too, with his little cream and green gardening can, filled too full and knocking against his legs and slopping water on his canvas shoes. I had the real watering can, my father's, though I could only carry it three-quarters full.

The foxes all had names, which were printed on a tin plate and hung beside their doors. They were not named when they were born, but when they survived the first year's pelting and were added to the breeding stock. Those my father had named were called names like Prince, Bob, Wally and Betty. Those I had named were called Star or Turk, or Maureen or Diana. Laird named one Maud after a hired girl we had when he was little, one Harold after a boy at school, and one Mexico, he did not say why.

Naming them did not make pets out of them, or anything like it. Nobody but my father ever went into the pens, and he had twice had blood-poisoning from bites. When I was bringing them their water they prowled up and down on the paths they had made inside their pens, barking seldom — they saved that for nighttime, when they might get up a chorus of community frenzy —but always watching me, their eyes burning, clear gold, in their pointed, malevolent faces. They were beautiful for their delicate legs and heavy, aristocratic tails and the bright fur sprinkled on dark down their backs — which gave them their name — but especially for their faces, drawn exquisitely sharp in pure hostility, and their golden eyes.

Besides carrying water I helped my father when he cut the long grass, and the lamb's quarter and flowering money-musk, that grew between the pens. He cut with the scythe and I raked into piles. Then he took a pitchfork and threw fresh-cut grass all over the top of the pens, to keep the foxes cooler and shade their coats, which were browned by too much sun. My father did not talk to me unless it was about the job we were doing. In this he was quite different from my mother, who, if she was feeling cheerful, would tell me all sorts of things — the name of a dog she had had when she was a little girl, the names of boys she had gone out with later on when she was grown up, and what certain dresses of hers had looked like — she could not imagine now what had become of them. Whatever thoughts and stories my father had were private, and I was shy of him and would never ask him questions. Nevertheless I worked willingly under his eyes, and with a feeling of pride. One time a feed salesman came down into the pens to talk to him and my father said, "Like to have you meet my new hired man." I turned away and raked furiously, red in the face with pleasure.

"Could of fooled me," said the salesman. "I thought it was only a girl."

After the grass was cut, it seemed suddenly much later in the year. I walked on stubble in the earlier evening, aware of the reddening skies, the entering silences, of fall. When I wheeled the tank out of the gate and put the padlock on, it was almost dark. One night at this time I saw my mother and father standing talking on the little rise of ground we called the gangway, in front of the barn. My father had just come from the meathouse; he had his stiff bloody apron on, and a pail of cut-up meat in his hand.

It was an odd thing to see my mother down at the barn. She did not often come out of the house unless it was to do something — hang out the wash or dig potatoes in the garden. She looked out of place, with her bare lumpy legs, not touched by the sun, her apron still on and damp across the stomach from the supper dishes. Her hair was tied up in a kerchief, wisps of it falling out. She would tie her hair up like this in the morning, saying she did not have time to do it properly, and it would stay tied up all day. It was true, too; she really did not have time. These days our back porch was piled with baskets of peaches and grapes and pears, bought in town, and onions and tomatoes and cucumbers grown at home, all waiting to be made into jelly and jam and preserves, pickles and chili sauce. In the kitchen there was a fire in the stove all day, jars clinked in boiling water, sometimes a cheesecloth bag was strung on a pole between two chairs, straining blue-black grape pulp for jelly. I was given jobs to do and I would sit at the table peeling peaches that had been soaked in the hot water, or cutting up onions, my eyes smarting and streaming. As soon as I was done I ran out of the house, trying to get out of earshot before my mother thought of what she wanted me to do next. I hated the hot dark kitchen in summer, the green blinds and the flypapers, the same old oilcloth table and wavy mirror and bumpy linoleum. My mother was too tired and preoccupied to talk to me, she had no heart to tell about the Normal School Graduation Dance; sweat trickled over her face and she was always counting under her breath, pointing at jars, dumping cups of sugar. It seemed to me that work in the house was endless, dreary and peculiarly depressing; work done out of doors, and in my father's service, was ritualistically important.

I wheeled the tank up to the barn, where it was kept, and I heard my mother saying, "Wait till Laird gets a little bigger, then you'll have a real help."

What my father said I did not hear. I was pleased by the way he stood listening, politely as he would to a salesman or a stranger, but with an air of wanting to get on with his real work. I felt my mother had no business down here and I wanted him to feel the same way. What did she mean about Laird? He was no help to anybody. Where was he now? Swinging himself sick on the swing, going around in circles, or trying to catch caterpillars. He never once stayed with me till I was finished.

"And then I can use her more in the house," I heard my mother say. She had a dead-quiet, regretful way of talking about me that always made me uneasy. "I just get my back turned and she runs off. It's not like I had a girl in the family at all."

I went and sat on a feed bag in the corner of the barn, not wanting to appear when this conversation was going on. My mother, I felt, was not to be trusted. She was kinder than my father and more easily fooled, but you could not depend on her, and the real reasons for the things she said and did were not to be known. She loved me, and she sat up late at night making a dress of the difficult style I wanted, for me to wear when school started, but she was also my enemy. She was always plotting. She was plotting now to get me to stay in the house more, although she knew I hated it (*because* she knew I hated it) and keep me from working for my father. It seemed to me she would do this simply out of perversity, and to try her power. It did not occur to me that she could be lonely, or jealous. No grown-up could be; they were too fortunate. I sat and kicked my heels monotonously against a feedbag, raising dust, and did not come out till she was gone.

At any rate, I did not expect my father to pay any attention to what she said. Who could imagine Laird doing my work — Laird remembering the padlock and cleaning out the watering-dishes with a leaf on the end of a stick, or even wheeling the tank without it tumbling over? It showed how little my mother knew about the way things really were.

I have forgotten to say what the foxes were fed. My father's bloody apron reminded me. They were fed horsemeat. At this time most farmers still kept horses, and when a horse got too old to work, or broke a leg or got down and would not get up, as they sometimes did, the owner would call my father, and he and Henry went out to the farm in the truck. Usually they shot and butchered the horse there, paying the farmer from five to twelve dollars. If they had already too much meat on hand, they would bring the horse back alive, and keep it for a few days or weeks in our stable, until the meat was needed. After the war the farmers were buying tractors and gradually getting rid of horses altogether, so it sometimes happened that we got a good healthy horse, that there was just no use for any more. If this happened in the winter we might keep the horse in our stable till spring, for we had plenty of hay and if there was a lot of snow — and the plow did not always get our road cleared — it was convenient to be able to go to town with a horse and cutter.

The winter I was eleven years old we had two horses in the stable. We did not know what names they had had before, so we called them Mack and Flora. Mack was an old black workhorse, sooty and indifferent. Flora was a sorrel mare, a driver. We took them both out in the cutter. Mack was slow and easy to handle. Flora was given to fits of violent alarm, veering at cars and even at other horses, but we loved her speed and high-stepping, her general air of gallantry and abandon. On Saturdays we went down to the stable and as soon as we opened the door on its cosy, animal-smelling darkness Flora threw up her head, rolled her eyes, whinnied despairingly and pulled herself through a crisis of nerves on the spot. It was not safe to go into her stall; she would kick.

This winter also I began to hear a great deal more on the theme my mother had sounded when she had been talking in front of the barn. I no longer felt safe. It seemed that in the minds of the people around me there was a steady undercurrent of thought, not to be deflected, on this one subject. The word *girl* had formerly seemed to me innocent and unburdened, like the word *child*; now it appeared that it was no such thing. A girl was not, as I had supposed, simply what I was; it was what I had to become. It was a definition, always touched with emphasis, with reproach and disappointment. Also it was a joke on me. Once Laird and I were fighting, and for the first time ever I had to use all my strength against him: even so, he caught and pinned my arm for a moment, really hurting me. Henry saw this, and laughed, saying, "Oh, that there Laird's gonna show you, one of these days!" Laird was getting a lot bigger. But I was getting bigger too.

My grandmother came to stay with us for a few weeks and I heard other things. "Girls don't slam doors like that." "Girls keep their knees together when they sit down." And worse still, when I asked some questions, "That's none of girls' business." I continued to slam the doors and sit as awkwardly as possible, thinking that by such measures I kept myself free.

When spring came, the horses were let out in the barnyard. Mack stood against the barn wall trying to scratch his neck and haunches, but Flora trotted up and down and reared at the fences, clattering her hooves against the rails. Snow drifts dwindled quickly, revealing the hard grey and brown earth, the familiar rise and fall of the ground, plain and bare after the fantastic landscape of winter. There was a great feeling of opening-out, of release. We just wore rubbers now, over our shoes; our feet felt ridiculously light. One Saturday we went out to the stable and found all the doors open, letting in the unaccustomed sunlight and fresh air. Henry was there, just idling around looking at his collection of calendars which were tacked up behind the stalls in a part of the stable my mother had probably never seen.

"Come to say goodbye to your old friend Mack?" Henry said. "Here, you give him a taste of oats." He poured some oats into Laird's cupped hands and Laird went to feed Mack. Mack's teeth were in bad shape. He ate very slowly, patiently shifting the oats around in his mouth, trying to find a stump of a molar to grind it on. "Poor old Mack," said Henry mournfully. "When a horse's teeth's gone, he's gone. That's about the way."

"Are you going to shoot him today?" I said. Mack and Flora had been in the stable so long I had almost forgotten they were going to be shot.

Henry didn't answer me. Instead he started to sing in a high, trembly, mocking-sorrowful voice, *Oh, there's no more work, for poor Uncle Ned, he's gone where the good darkies go.* Mack's thick, blackish tongue worked diligently at Laird's hand. I went out before the song was ended and sat down on the gangway.

I had never seen them shoot a horse, but I knew where it was done. Last summer Laird and I had come upon a horse's entrails before they were buried. We had thought it was a big black snake, coiled up in the sun. That was around in the field that ran up beside the barn. I thought that if we went inside the barn, and found a wide crack or a knothole to look through, we would be able to see them do it. It was not something I wanted to see; just the same, if a thing really happened, it was better to see it, and know.

My father came down from the house, carrying the gun. "What are you doing here?" he said.

"Nothing."

"Go on up and play around the house."

He sent Laird out of the stable. I said to Laird, "Do you want to see them shoot Mack?" and without waiting for an answer led him around to the front door of the barn, opened it carefully, and went in. "Be quiet or they'll hear us," I said. We could hear Henry and my father talking in the stable, then the heavy, shuffling steps of Mack being backed out of his stall.

In the loft it was cold and dark. Thin, crisscrossed beams of sunlight fell through the cracks. The hay was low. It was a rolling country, hills and hollows, slipping under our feet. About four feet up was a beam going around the walls. We piled hay up in one corner and I boosted Laird up and hoisted myself. The beam was not very wide; we crept along it with our hands flat on the barn walls. There were plenty of knotholes, and I found one that gave me the view I wanted — a corner of the barnyard, the gate, part of the field. Laird did not have a knothole and began to complain.

I showed him a widened crack between two boards. "Be quiet and wait. If they hear you you'll get us in trouble."

My father came in sight carrying the gun. Henry was leading Mack by the halter. He dropped it and took out his cigarette papers and tobacco; he rolled cigarettes for my father and himself. While this was going on Mack nosed around in the old, dead grass along the fence. Then my father opened the gate and they took Mack through. Henry led Mack way from the path to a patch of ground and they talked together, not loud enough for us to hear. Mack again began searching for a mouthful of fresh grass, which was not to be found. My father walked away in a straight line, and stopped short at a distance which seemed to suit him. Henry was walking away from Mack too, but sideways, still negligently holding on to the halter. My father raised the gun and Mack looked up as if he had noticed something and my father shot him.

Mack did not collapse at once but swayed, lurched sideways and fell, first on his side; then he rolled over on his back and, amazingly, kicked his legs for a few seconds in the air. At this Henry laughed, as if Mack had done a trick for him. Laird, who had drawn a long, groaning breath of surprise when the shot was fired, said out loud, "He's not dead." And it seemed to me it might be true. But his legs stopped, he rolled on his side again, his muscles quivered and sank. The two men walked over and looked at him in a businesslike way; they bent down and examined his forehead where the bullet had gone in, and now I saw his blood on the brown grass.

"Now they just skin him and cut him up," I said. "Let's go." My legs were a little shaky and I jumped gratefully down into the hay. "Now you've seen how they shoot a horse," I said in a congratulatory way, as if I had seen it many times before. "Let's see if any barn cat's had kittens in the hay." Laird jumped. He seemed young and obedient again. Suddenly I remembered how, when he was little, I had brought him into the barn and told him to climb the ladder to the top beam. That was in the spring, too, when the hay was low. I had done it out of a need for excitement, a desire for something to happen so that I could tell about it. He was wearing a little bulky brown and white checked coat, made down from one of mine. He went all the way up, just as I told him, and sat down on the top beam with the hay far below him on one side, and the barn floor and some old machinery on the other. Then I ran screaming to my father, "Laird's up on the top beam!" My father came, my mother came, my father went up the ladder talking very quietly and brought Laird down under his arm, at which my mother leaned against the ladder and began to cry. They said to me, "Why weren't you watching him?" but nobody ever knew the truth. Laird did not know enough to tell. But whenever I saw the brown and white checked coat hanging in the closet, or at the bottom of the rag bag, which was where it ended up, I felt a weight in my stomach, the sadness of unexorcized guilt.

I looked at Laird who did not even remember this, and I did not like the look on this thin, winter-pale face. His expression was not frightened or upset, but remote, concentrating. "Listen," I said, in an unusually bright and friendly voice, "you aren't going to tell, are you?"

"No," he said absently.

"Promise."

"Promise," he said. I grabbed the hand behind his back to make sure he was not crossing his fingers. Even so, he might have a nightmare; it might come out that way. I decided I had better work hard to get all thoughts of what he had seen out of his mind — which, it seemed to me, could not hold very many things at a time. I got some money I had saved and that afternoon we went into Jubilee and saw a show, with Judy Canova, at which we both laughed a great deal. After that I thought it would be all right.

Two weeks later I knew they were going to shoot Flora. I knew from the night before, when I heard my mother ask if the hay was holding out all right, and my father said, "Well, after to-morrow there'll just be the cow, and we should be able to put her out to grass in another week." So I knew it was Flora's turn in the morning.

This time I didn't think of watching it. That was something to see just one time. I had not thought about it very often since, but sometimes when I was busy, working at school, or standing in front of the mirror combing my hair and wondering if I would be pretty when I grew up, the whole scene would flash into my mind: I would see the easy, practised way my father raised the gun, and hear Henry laughing when Mack kicked his legs in the air. I did not have any great feeling of horror and opposition, such as a city child might have had; I was too used to seeing the death of animals as a necessity by which we lived. Yet I felt a little ashamed, and there was a new wariness, a sense of holding-off, in my attitude to my father and his work.

It was a fine day, and we were going around the yard picking up tree branches that had been torn off in winter storms. This was something we had been told to do, and also we wanted to use them to make a teepee. We heard Flora whinny, and then my father's voice and Henry's shouting, and we ran down to the barnyard to see what was going on.

The stable door was open. Henry had just brought Flora out, and she had broken away from him. She was running free in the barnyard, from one end to the other. We climbed up on the fence. It was exciting to see her running, whinnying, going up on her hind legs, prancing and threatening like a horse in a Western movie, an unbroken ranch horse, though she was just an old driver, an old sorrel mare. My father and Henry ran after her and tried to grab the dangling halter. They tried to work her into a corner, and they had almost succeeded when she made a run between them, wild-eyed, and disappeared around the corner of the barn. We heard the rails clatter down as she got over the fence, and Henry yelled, "She's into the field now!"

That meant she was in the long L-shaped field that ran up by the house. If she got around the center, heading towards the lane, the gate was open; the truck had been driven into the field this morning. My father shouted to me, because I was on the other side of the fence, nearest the lane, "Go shut the gate!"

I could run very fast. I ran across the garden, past the tree where our swing was hung, and jumped across a ditch into the lane. There was the open gate. She had not got out, I could not see her up on the road; she must have run to the other end of the field. The gate was heavy. I lifted it out of the gravel and carried it across the roadway. I had it half-way across when she came in sight, galloping straight towards me. There was just time to get the chain on. Laird came scrambling through the ditch to help me.

Instead of shutting the gate, I opened it as wide as I could. I did not make any decision to do this, it was just what I did. Flora never slowed down; she galloped straight past me, and Laird jumped up and down, yelling, "Shut it, shut it!" even after it was too late. My father and Henry appeared in the field a moment too late to see what I had done. They only saw Flora heading for the township road. They would think I had not got there in time.

They did not waste any time asking about it. They went back to the barn and got the gun and the knives they used, and put these in the truck; then they turned the truck around and came bouncing up the field toward us. Laird called to them, "Let me go too, let me go too!" and Henry stopped the truck and they took him in. I shut the gate after they were all gone.

I supposed Laird would tell. I wondered what would happen to me. I had never disobeyed my father before, and I could not understand why I had done it. Flora would not really get away. They would catch up with her in the truck. Or if they did not catch her this morning somebody would see her and telephone us this afternoon or tomorrow. There was no wild country here for her to run to, only farms. What was more, my father had paid for her, we needed the meat to feed the foxes, we needed the foxes to make our living. All I had done was make more work for my father who worked hard enough already. And when my father found out about it he was not going to trust me any more; he would know that I was not entirely on his side. I was on Flora's side, and that made me no use to anybody, not even to her. Just the same, I did not regret it; when she came running at me and I held the gate open, that was the only thing I could do.

I went back to the house, and my mother said, "What's all the commotion?" I told her that Flora had kicked down the fence and got away. "Your poor father," she said, "now he'll have to go chasing over the countryside. Well, there isn't any use planning dinner before one." She put up the ironing board. I wanted to tell her, but thought better of it and went upstairs and sat on my bed.

Lately I had been trying to make my part of the room fancy,

spreading the bed with old lace curtains, and fixing myself a dressing-table with some leftovers of cretonne for a skirt. I planned to put up some kind of barricade between my bed and Laird's, to keep my section separate from his. In the sunlight, the lace curtains were just dusty rags. We did not sing at night any more. One night when I was singing Laird said, "You sound silly," and I went right on but the next night I did not start. There was not so much need to anyway, we were no longer afraid. We knew it was just old furniture over there, old jumble and confusion. We did not keep to the rules. I still stayed awake after Laird was asleep and told myself stories, but even in these stories something different was happening, mysterious alterations took place. A story might start off in the old way, with a spectacular danger, a fire or wild animals, and for a while I might rescue people; then things would change around, and instead, somebody would be rescuing me. It might be a boy from our class at school, or even Mr. Campbell, our teacher, who tickled girls under the arms. And at this point the story concerned itself at great length with what I looked like — how long my hair was, and what kind of dress I had on; by the time I had these details worked out the real excitement of the story was lost.

It was later than one o'clock when the truck came back. The tarpaulin was over the back, which meant there was meat in it. My mother had to heat dinner up all over again. Henry and my father had changed from their bloody overalls into ordinary working overalls in the barn, and they washed their arms and necks and faces at the sink, and splashed water on their hair and combed it. Laird lifted his arm to show off a streak of blood. "We shot old Flora," he said, "and cut her up in fifty pieces."

"Well I don't want to hear about it," my mother said. "And don't come to my table like that."

My father made him go and wash the blood off.

We sat down and my father said grace and Henry pasted his chewing-gum on the end of his fork, the way he always did; when he took it off he would have us admire the pattern. We began to pass the bowls of steaming, overcooked vegetables. Laird looked across the table at me and said proudly, distinctly. "Anyway it was her fault Flora got away."

"What?" my father said.

"She could of shut the gate and she didn't. She just open' it up and Flora run out."

"Is that right?" my father said.

Everybody at the table was looking at me. I nodded, swallowing food with great difficulty. To my shame, tears flooded my eyes.

My father made a curt sound of disgust. "What did you do that for?"

I did not answer. I put down my fork and waited to be sent from the table, still not looking up.

But this did not happen. For some time nobody said anything, then Laird said matter-of-factly, "She's crying."

"Never mind," my father said. He spoke with resignation, even good humour, the words which absolved and dismissed me for good. "She's only a girl," he said.

I didn't protest that, even in my heart. Maybe it was true.

A Sick Call

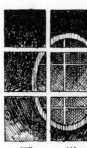

Mrs. Bruce was an old friend who had been sick for a long time, the children's mother told them. After supper they were to take her a little gift of fresh milk and wild strawberries.

The milk, brought warm and sweet from the barn, was strained through a white cotton cloth and the berries were washed in spring water. The girl was given a quart lard-kettle full of milk, and the boy, who was two years younger, was given a quart lard-kettle half-full of berries.

They went off together across fields where there were crows, mushrooms and innumerable brown cakes of cow manure, along railroad tracks bordered with blackberry bushes, where the smell of coal hung in the air, and down a path that wound cool and dark as a tunnel through a forest of birch and juniper.

The girl carried herself very primly as she often did when she and the boy were sent on an errand together. At such times she was very much aware of the two years that separated them.

"Be careful. You'll spill the berries," she kept telling the boy.

ALDEN
NOWLAN

82

"What will she look like?" the boy asked her. "Mrs. Bruce, I mean."

"She'll look sick, silly. How would you expect her to look?"

He swung his kettle harder and higher.

"I know that," he said. "I mean what do people look like when they're sick. Real sick. When they're going to die."

"You'll spill those berries if you're not careful. Oh, I don't know. They look scared, I guess. Everybody I ever saw who was real sick looked scared."

"What are they scared of?"

"How should I know. Maybe they're not scared of anything. Maybe they just look that way. Watch what you're doing with that kettle. And don't ask so many silly questions."

It was beginning to be dusk and the whistling of the birds had changed, as it always changes at dusk. In the daylight, each bird seems to sing for itself, or they call to one another across great distances. But at dusk they gather in flocks, each species separate, and sing strange sad songs together.

"I wonder what it's like to die," the boy said. "Maybe I'll get sick and die. Kids die sometimes."

"Don't you talk about dying in front of Mrs. Bruce or I'll tell Mum and she'll skin you alive."

They came to a wire fence. The boy climbed over it, while the girl crawled under. They were self-conscious about these little acts that emphasized the difference between them. The girl resented the convention that required her to crawl under fences, yet would have been ashamed to climb over. On the other side she scolded the boy violently for spilling a handful of berries.

Not far beyond the fence stood a white cottage, the home of the sick woman. Its windows, hung with white lace curtains, were orange with the reflection of the setting sun. There was a rosebush by the door and a water pump in the yard.

The boy stopped.

"You take the berries. I'll wait here," he mumbled.

But he could not stand her look of scorn and triumph as she

reached to take the kettle from him. He drew it back and when she strode toward the cottage he plodded after her.

It was not necessary for them to enter the cottage. The sick woman lay on a hospital bed on an open porch. There were screens to keep out blackflies and mosquitoes. Her visitors stood outdoors and talked with her through the screens.

"Hello, Mrs. Bruce," the girl said.

The sick woman gazed out at them. Her skin was chalky white except for her cheeks, which were red as from a slap.

"We brought you something," the girl said, her voice quavering faintly.

The sick woman continued to stare at them with eyes that contained neither understanding nor curiosity. Stretching out a claw-like hand, she took a paper cup from a cluttered table beside her bed.

"We're the O'Brien children," the girl explained. "Judd and Mary's kids."

Then a horrible thing happened.

The sick woman spat into the paper cup — an obscene red and yellow blob of phlegm and blood.

She wiped her lips with a handkerchief.

"Yes, of course," she said, "You're Kevin and Stephanie. Stephanie, you're a very pretty little girl. And Kevin you look exactly like your father, except you have your mother's eyes. Come closer. Let me see you."

"We brought you some strawberries," the girl said. "And some milk."

She held up her lard-kettle so the sick woman could see it and motioned for the boy to do the same.

"Yes. Thank your mother for me. It was nice of her to remember. Not many people remember anymore. Come closer. Open the screens a little, boy. I want to see you."

Kevin could not take his eyes off the paper cup.

"Yes, you are handsome children," the sick woman said. "So pretty both of you, although I don't suppose boys like being called pretty, Kevin, do they, but you are pretty both of

you, so pretty and so young, so very, very young. Would you
like some grapes, I have some here — "

She reached for a bowl on the bedside table, but the effort
made her cough and her hand came back not with the bowl
but with the paper cup. She spat again.

"I want to go home, Stevie," Kevin said.

"We have to go now, Mrs. Bruce," Stephanie said.

She lifted the kettle of milk through the opening in the
screens and sat it on the windowsill. Quickly, Kevin placed his
kettle beside hers.

The sick woman took his hand.

The boy tried to pull away, but her grip was astonishingly
strong.

"Let go of me," Kevin whimpered. "Stevie, make her let go
of me."

"Don't be such a ninny, Kevin," Stephanie said. "You be
nice to Mrs. Bruce or I'll tell on you when we get home. You
see if I don't."

There was no warmth in the sick woman's fingers. She
tightened her grip and drew the boy closer.

"You're not afraid of me, are you, boy?" she said.

She laughed harshly, coughed again and spat once more
into the paper cup.

"No," he whispered. "But you're hurting me."

"Nonsense. A sick old woman like me can't hurt a big,
healthy boy like you."

She laughed again and released his hand. He took a deep
breath and put both hands in the pockets of his jeans.

"You're both so young and pretty," the sick woman said.
"Do you know that I was once as young and pretty as you?"

"No!" Kevin cried — and then blushed at his own
stupidity.

"Oh, yes! I was young and pretty and wore red slippers and
danced with the soldiers. And, before that, I played games,
just as you do now. I played London Bridge and Ring Around
the Rosies and Hop-Scotch, and I rode a bright blue bicycle

with ribbons on its handlebars, and I ran and ran and ran, oh, how I ran, I could run faster than most boys, faster than any girl in Lockhartville, you should have seen me run, then. And it's just like it was yesterday. Do you know it seems like it was only yesterday, I was just like you?"

"Are you coming, Stevie, or will I go home without you?" Kevin growled.

"Wait!" cried the sick woman. "Listen! You won't believe me, but do you know that tomorrow you'll be like me! Yes, tomorrow! That's how quickly it all happens. You're born and the next day you die. Just one day of life that's all that any of us has — "

"We have to go home," Stephanie said. "It's almost dark." The sick woman smiled sadly.

"I shouldn't be talking such nonsense," she said. "You're quite right. It's getting dark. You'd better go now."

The children ran most of the way home. It was dark now and neither of them felt quite safe until they came in sight of their home, lights gleaming from the kitchen windows and the open door of the barn.

"I hate her," Kevin said at one point. "She's an old witch."

"Don't talk like that," Stephanie warned him, but without much conviction in her voice.

"The way she spit in that cup! She's an old witch and God is punishing her for all the bad things she's done."

"Don't be such a baby. There's no such thing as witches."

"If she's not a witch, then she's a real bad woman or else God wouldn't be punishing her like that. God wouldn't make anybody good spit like that. He wouldn't. He wouldn't. He wouldn't."

"It's no use talking to you. You're such a baby," Stephanie said.

Three months later Mrs. Bruce died. The children's parents went to the funeral, Mary in the black dress she wore to church every Sunday, Judd wearing the only white shirt and necktie he owned.

When they came home, they sat for a long time in the kitchen, still wearing their best clothes, and talked of the dead woman. The children listened quietly, cowed by the mysterious rituals of death.

"What will Clint do now, do you suppose?" Mary wondered.

"Oh, get married again, I shouldn't wonder. He's not an old man yet, Clint isn't."

"Lucinda has been a trial to him, there's no doubt of that. But they say God never gives us a burden without giving us the strength to bear it."

"Well, she's better off the way she is. It's a big load lifted from Clint's shoulders and she's out of her misery. Like I was telling Rupe Barkhouse, you couldn't really feel sad at that funeral." *Conclusion*

"She was a good woman," Mary sighed.

"One of the best," Judd agreed.

"I'm glad she's dead, she was a bad woman," said Kevin loudly.

"Kevin!" his mother cried.

And for a long moment the two adults stared at the boy, speechless with a bewilderment that transformed itself, very slowly, into anger. *Conclusion*

Shoes For Dancing

"Eek! Don't expose me!" Sally shrieked in mock alarm.

As usual, Miss Collins was threatening to whisk off the cotton sheet that protected Sally's fifteen year old body from the scrutiny of the other patients on the ward. She never carried out the threat, and Sally knew she wouldn't but it was part of a ritual: the move to snatch away the covering, the shriek of protest, the stay of execution.

Sally realized she was perhaps being a bit ridiculous, overly modest under the circumstances. The rest of the patients, females from four to sixty, certainly did not seem to care who saw what parts of their anatomy. But after nearly two years in hospital, Sally still washed and dressed under the bedclothes.

Miss Collins prepared to change the dressings on Sally's leg and shoulder.

"That bone is coming out today!" she announced dramatically, waving a pair of forceps in the air. A splinter of decayed bone had been trying for days to work its way out through the flesh below Sally's knee.

GERALDINE
RUBIA

Half fearful that Miss Collins' hand

would slip, Sally tensed every muscle. She need not have worried. As always, the nurse worked gently, tugging and jiggling the bone so that it would move an imperceptible distance on its journey. She had to be very careful, for the surrounding flesh was raw and tender, and the fugitive bone jagged and sharp.

As she worked, they made jokes that were grim, if not horrible, to the uninitiated.

"What will we do with this when it comes out?"

"It might make a good false tooth . . ."

"Or a charm for a bracelet . . ."

"If we can save enough pieces, we might even make a pot of soup."

Then, unbelievably, the bone was out. Sally had been prepared for a final tearing pain, but there was the two inch splinter in the forceps; the rotting symbol of months of suffering. Now this wound would begin to heal but already the dreary process was beginning again. Lately, there had been a dull ache, this time in her left arm, which always announced the gathering of another abscess on yet another bone. Soon her temperature would soar, her appetite would vanish, and life would be acutely miserable until the noxious cargo was unloaded.

The nurse finished the dressings quickly, and stayed a minute, to see the latest additions to Sally's scrapbook.

"Do the task that's nearest . . ."

"If you think you are beaten, you are . . ."

Sally told her that these had been brought by one of the patients from the men's ward.

"They're always bringing me verses about love and sunsets and mothers, and try, try again."

"Isn't that what you like? I thought you told me your very favorite poem is this one on the first page, and it's all about love."

But she hadn't told Miss Collins why that was her favorite. It was something Ron had quoted, and she had gone to the trouble of finding the entire poem so that it could have the place of honor in her scrapbook.

She had met Ron at a parish garden party two years before; dark-haired, brown-eyed, good looking Ron. They liked each other instantly, and had spent the afternoon wandering around the grounds talking and laughing together. He talked easily, sure of himself, but not a show-off. There was a special word to describe him ... debonair, that was it; so different from the rough and ready boys she went to school with.

They were both too young for dates, at least Sally was, yet they talked of meeting again. She had not seen him since, for she had been admitted to hospital soon afterwards, but he was never long out of her mind. Several times she had started to write him, knowing she would never dare to mail the letter. She imagined a thousand times over what it would be like to be his girl: to walk with him, talk with him, dance with him.

Of course she would not kiss him until they were sure they really loved each other.

"A little of that sentimental stuff is all right, but I'd rather something humorous. There's a good one by Ogden Nash that I cut out of a magazine, or I tried writing a limerick myself, but I'm afraid it's not very good."

The nurse thought Sally's limerick showed considerable talent.

"That's marvellous, Sally. I didn't know you were a poet. Imagine, when you become famous, I can say I knew you when."

Smiling, she went on to her next patient.

Sally got out her school books to finish her "homework" for the teacher who would spend fifteen minutes with her in the afternoon. She had liked school, and regretted the year that had passed without instruction before a teacher was appointed to the hospital. It wasn't easy to study on the ward with children crying, women shouting conversation from bed to bed, and radios blaring on different stations, but she was making some progress.

"Who wants mail this morning?"

Sally was surprised when the orderly passed her a letter. Her family lived near enough to visit her often, and she did not receive many letters. She looked at the signature first, and could hardly believe her eyes. It was from Ron!

She read the letter quickly, self-consciously, as if the entire ward were reading over her shoulder.

... can't help thinking about you ... not able to forget ... heard you are in hospital ... could lend you some books ... will come soon ... fun we will have ... dancing when you're well again ...

"Sally, can you show me how to do this sum?"

Joan was coming down the ward in her wheelchair; sophisticated, seventeen year old Joan. If she ever saw Ron's letter, everyone in the hospital would know about it and there would be no end to the teasing. It would spoil everything. Sally quickly tore the letter into tiny pieces and stuffed them into the paper bag clipped to the side of her bed, but she was not quick enough to escape Joan's sharp eye.

"Why did you tear up your letter? You hardly had time to read it."

"Oh, it's nothing important. Just some old nonsense."

"Who was it from? It must be a boy-friend. You're blushing as red as a beet."

Joan was peering into the paper bag by this time, but the scraps of the letter had settled in among orange peels and candy papers and inquisitive as she was, Joan did not attempt to rescue the mysterious note.

"You certainly like to keep things to yourself, don't you?"

"It's really nothing interesting. What about that sum you're doing?"

Sally took Joan's book and tried to explain the arithmetic problem. Joan did not like schoolwork but could not very well avoid it, since she had let it be understood by the other patients that the teacher had been engaged especially for her. She had been in the hospital even longer than Sally and her main interests in life were doing up her face and hair, and flirting with the interns and orderlies. The two girls struggled through the arithmetic session and came out of it without fighting, but just barely. Sally wondered again why she had ever thought she wanted to be a teacher. But then, there could not be many pupils like Joan.

Sally's usual practice on weekday mornings was to hurry through her lessons so that she would have time to read awhile before dinner.

She read almost everything that came to hand. Murder mysteries. Ghost stories. Once there had been a book on theology. Not very complicated, Sally had thought, until a visiting nun had asked her whether it was not a little deep for her age.

One novel she had opened at random, only to shut it again quickly after one puzzling but somehow frightening sentence. Whether she thought it was forbidden for her to know what the words signified, or whether she was afraid to find out, she could not tell.

She sensed it had something to do with sex, a subject that had never been mentioned at home although she was already thirteen when she came to the hospital. And considering the number and types of patients who had come and gone since, she had learned surprisingly little. She would never ask, and what she overheard was only the vaguest of phrases. "When I get home with Jack again, oh what a night that will be!" She knew the woman did not mean an evening of playing cards or dancing.

Today she was beginning another story about an English boarding school for girls, big strapping Lacrosse-playing girls whose worst misfortune was spraining an ankle while on a paper chase. And their prim, incredible school mistresses. "It is deplorable that a child of your age should be so colossally ignorant." Did they really talk like that?

Though her eyes were on the book, Sally's thoughts were far removed from the girls' boarding school. Mentally, she was re-reading Ron's letter and feeling disgusted with herself for tearing it up. She wished she could read it over and over, savoring every word. She had read it too quickly to remember everything, and now the pages were in such little pieces that they could never be put back together again. She supposed she hadn't dreamt it all. No, she still had the envelope and that blessed, wonderful feeling that no amount of dreaming could possibly give. How many times she had imagined something like this happening and now she would soon see him again.

One phrase jumped out from the confusion of phrases that she remembered . . . dancing when you're well again.

Before the trouble had started in her foot, Sally used to improvise swooping, swaying, dipping dances with her father just for the fun of feeling and following the music, any kind of music. Would she ever dance like that again . . . dance with Ron?

Suddenly she decided that today she would ask her doctor about getting a special shoe. Her foot was enlarged out of proportion and would not get into any ordinary shoe. Maybe a special one could be made in the hospital's brace shop. She had been thinking about it for a long time, but hesitated to make a suggestion to the doctor. Well, she was not going to put it off any longer.

After the noon meal, there was a rest hour, but Sally did not sleep. She could only think of Ron and how good it would be to see him again. She pictured how it would be on his first visit. They would talk as easily as if they had seen each other only yesterday, but there would be so much more to talk about. And maybe, when the infection in her bones cleared up and she had proper shoes, maybe they could go dancing some day. Nothing fast, just slow dances, but it would be wonderful just the same.

Rest hour ended with the blaring of a radio and a burst of talk from practically all the patients at once. Some of the older girls started comparing their bust measurements and Sally pretended not to notice as she picked up her knitting. Before the doctor came, and then the teacher, she could do a few rounds on the sweater she was knitting for the baby brother she had not seen yet.

"How about you, Sally? How big are you?" As usual, Joan was the ringleader.

"I don't know. Not very big."

"Let's have a look."

"Don't be so foolish."

"Oh, come on. Open up your bed jacket. It's not going to hurt, is it?"

After several minutes of this, Sally let herself be persuaded to reveal her small, firm breasts, thinking that after all they were quite presentable. She regretted it instantly.

"Good Lord! What were you trying to hide? Sure you have nothing there at all!"

This in a pleasant, friendly tone, for they probably thought of her as only a baby. She could not be angry, but she felt shamed and inadequate, and her natural modesty would now be reinforced for a new reason.

Suddenly the patients hushed as the doctor came in to make his rounds. He soon reached Sally's bed and made the usual inquiry, expecting the "Fine, thank you" which she would undoubtedly answer even if she were dying. He looked surprised when she blurted out her question, and his answer had a tone of amused tolerance.

"A shoe? You're worried about a shoe? My dear child you should consider yourself damn lucky to have a foot." Without further comment, he went on to the next patient.

Consider yourself damn lucky to have a foot. Sally repeated the words to herself, checking to see if they came out at an even number. This was a new habit she had acquired. Sometimes she found herself rearranging her thoughts into sentences with an even number of words. When she first noticed herself doing this she was mystified, slightly alarmed. Finally she had decided it was the result of all the knitting she had been doing, the endless counting of stitches. Cast on a multiple of four. Cast on a multiple of four plus two. Cast on an even number. Consider yourself damn lucky to have a foot.

A misshapen, ugly lump that would not even bear her weight. Her father had said to her once that it should have been amputated, but the doctor said it was better to have a defective natural limb than an artificial one. And after all, the doctors know best.

If all the abscesses healed and no new ones came, at least she could go home. She could walk on crutches. If she didn't get better, if the infection kept on striking at all the bones in her body, over and over . . . she had one of her moments of panic at the thought of dying, and then she remembered about Ron.

She couldn't talk to anyone else about her discouragements and fears, least of all her parents because they worried enough about her as it was, but now she would have someone to confide in. Ron would understand and reassure her, and they would laugh all her worries away.

But Ron knew only that she was in hospital. He probably imagined her whizzing around glamorously in a wheelchair, like Joan. How would he feel when he saw that awful foot? What if there was really to be no end to the abscesses?

The teacher came and somehow Sally got through the lesson. Then it was visiting time and her father came. He was working night shift this week.

He put a couple of books on the bed, and Sally noticed the smell of beer. He usually stopped for one on the way to see her.

"Well, Miss, how are you feeling today?"

"Fine. I had an ache in my arm, but I forgot about it for a while when I was reading."

"It can't be too bad, if you were able to forget about it."

This annoyed her, because the ache was real and any relief was slight and temporary. At the same time, she realized that her father needed to believe she was not actually suffering.

"I wonder how much longer you'll have to stay here. I

always said the leg should come off. You would have been better by now."

"Look, Dad, the doctors know what they're doing."

She diverted him with questions about her sisters' progress in school and their reactions to the new baby, all the time feeling guilty because she wanted him to go so she could think about Ron.

When at last he did go, Sally found that instead of attempting to sort out her thoughts, she was reaching for pen and paper.

The letter was soon finished and she gave it to a nurse going off duty to post. It was brief, appreciative, and polite. When Ron read it, he would know that he was not to come and see her.

She picked up the book about the English girls' boarding school and tried to read. She had to keep from crying, for somebody would be sure to notice.

... it is deplorable that a child of your age ... consider yourself damn lucky ... my God, please let me be all right ...

The Skating Party

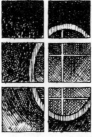

Our house looked down on the lake. From the east windows you could see it: a long sickle of blue, its banks hung with willow. Beyond was a wooded ridge, which, like all such ridges in our part of the country, ran from northeast to southwest.

In another part of the world, both lake and ridge would have had names. Here, only people had names. I was Maida; my father was Will, my mother was Winnie. Take us all together and we were the Singletons. The Will Singletons, that is, as opposed to the Dan Singletons, who were my grandparents and dead, or Nathan Singleton, who was my uncle and lived in the city.

In the books I read, lakes and hills had names, and so did ponds and houses. Their names made them more real to me, of greater importance, than the hills and lakes and sloughs that I saw every day. I was eleven years old before I learned that the hill on which our house was built had once had a name. It was called Stone Man Hill. My parents had never thought to tell me that.

It was my uncle, Nathan Singleton,

MERNA
SUMMERS

97

who told me. Uncle Nathan was a bachelor. He had been a teacher before he came to Willow Bunch, but he had wanted to be a farmer. He had farmed for a few years when he was a young man, on a quarter that was now part of our farm. His quarter was just south of what had been my grandfather's home place, and was now ours. But then he had moved to the city and become a teacher again.

In some ways it seemed as if he had never really left Willow Bunch. He spent all his holidays at our place, taking walks with me, talking to my mother, helping my father with such chores as he hadn't lost the knack of performing. Our home was his home. I found it hard to imagine him as I knew he must be in his classroom: wearing a suit, chalk dust on his sleeve, putting seat work on the blackboard. He didn't even talk like a teacher.

Uncle Nathan was older than my father, quite a lot older, but he didn't seem so to me. In some ways he seemed younger, for he told me things and my father did not. Not that my father was either silent or unloving. He talked as much as anybody, and he was fond of some people — me included — and showed it. What he did not give away was information.

Some children are sensitive: an eye and an ear and a taking-in of subtleties. I wasn't like that. I wanted to be told. I wanted to know how things really were and how people really acted. Sometimes it seemed to me that collecting the facts was uphill work. I persisted because it was important for me to have them. I wanted to know who to praise and who to blame. Until I was in my mid-teens, that didn't seem to me to be too much to ask.

Perhaps my father had a reluctance to look at things too closely himself. He wanted to like people, and he may have found it easier to do if he kept them a little out of focus. Besides that, he believed that life was something that children should be protected from knowing about for as long as possible.

I got most of my information from my mother. She believed that knowledge *was* protection: that children had a right to know and parents had an obligation to teach. She didn't know all there was to know, but what she did know she intended to pass on to me.

I knew this because I heard her say so one night after I had gone to bed. Uncle Nathan, who was at the farm for the weekend, saw things my mother's way. "What you don't know *can* hurt you," he said. "Especially what you don't know about yourself."

So my mother and my uncle talked to me, both as a sort of innoculation against life and because, I now believe, both of them liked to talk anyway. I was always willing to listen. My father listened too. He might feel that my mother told me too much, but his conviction wasn't strong enough to stop her.

It was Uncle Nathan, talking for pleasure, not policy, who gave me the pleasure of knowing that I lived in a place with a name. Stone Man Hill was so named, he said, because long ago there had existed on the slopes below our house the shape of a man, outlined in fieldstones.

"He was big," Uncle Nathan said. "Maybe fifteen yards, head to foot."

It was a summer afternoon. I was eleven. My father, in from the fields for coffee, was sitting at the kitchen table. His eyelashes were sooty with field dust. My mother was perched on a kitchen stool by the cupboard, picking over berries.

"He must have been quite a sight," my father said.

I walked to the east window of the kitchen and looked out, trying to imagine our hillside field of brome as unbroken prairie sod, trying to picture what a stone man would look like stretched out among the buffalo beans and gopher holes, his face to the sky.

"You get me a writing pad and I'll show you what he looked like," Uncle Nathan said.

I got the pad and Uncle Nathan sat down at the table opposite my father. I sat beside him, watching as he began to trace a series of dots. His hand worked quickly, as if the dots were already visible, but only to his eyes. The outline of a man took shape.

"Who made the stone man?" I asked.

"Indians," Uncle Nathan said. He held the picture up, as if considering additions. "But I don't know when and I don't know why."

"He could have been there a hundred years," my father said. "Maybe more. There was no way of telling."

"I used to wonder why the Indians chose this hill," Uncle Nathan said. "I still do."

He got up and walked to the window, looking out at the hill and the lake and the ridge. "It may be that it was some sort of holy place to them," he said.

My mother left the cupboard and came across to the table. She picked up Uncle Nathan's drawing. Looking at it, the corners of her mouth twitched upwards.

"You're sure you haven't forgotten anything?" she asked. "Your mother used to say that the stone man was *very* complete."

Uncle Nathan returned her smile. "The pencil's right here, Winnie," he said. "You're welcome to it."

My father spoke quickly. "It was too bad the folks didn't have a camera," he said. "It would have been nice to have a picture of the stone man."

My mother went back to her berries.

"I've always been sorry I was too young to remember him," my father said. "Before he turned into a rock pile, that is."

I hadn't yet got around to wondering about the stone man's disappearance. Now I did. He should still have been on his hillside for me to look at. My father had been a baby when his people came to Willow Bunch, and he couldn't remember the stone man. My uncle had been a young man and could. But the difference in their ages and experience hadn't kept them from sharing a feeling of excitement at the thought of a stone man on our hillside. Why had my grandfather been insensible to this appeal? Hadn't he liked the stone man?

"Liking wouldn't enter into it," my father said. "Your grandfather had a family to feed. He knew where his duty lay."

"There was 30 acres broke when Pa bought this place,"
Uncle Nathan said. "He thought he needed more. And this
hill was the only land he could break without brushing it
first."

Somebody else had owned our place before my grandfather,
hadn't they? I asked. He hadn't turned the stone man into a
rock pile.

"He was a bachelor," my father said.

"The way your grandfather saw it," Uncle Nathan said, "it
was a case of wheat or stones. And he chose wheat."

"Which would you have chosen?" I asked Uncle Nathan.
"Which did you want?"

"I wanted both," Uncle Nathan said.

"The choice wasn't yours to make." My mother spoke as if
she were defending him.

"That's what I thought then," Uncle Nathan said. "I
thought when Pa told me to get those rocks picked, that that
was what I had to do. I think now I should have spoken up. I
know for years I felt guilty whenever I remembered that I had
done just what was expected of me."

He looked up, a half-smile on his face. "I know it sounds
crazy," he said, "but I felt as if the stone man had more claim
on me than my own father did."

"We all of us think some crazy things sometimes," my
father said.

From my point of view, Uncle Nathan had only one
peculiarity. He had never married. And though I sometimes
asked him why, I never found any satisfaction in his answers.

"Maybe it wasn't every girl who took my eye," he told me
once. "I'd pity the girl who had to count on me to take care of
her," he said another time.

Then my mother told me about the skating party. It had
been a dark night in November, and my mother, five years
old, had come to our lake with her parents, and spent the
night pushing a kitchen chair in front of her across the ice,
trying to learn to skate. The party was being held in honour of

Uncle Nathan and a girl called Eunice Lathem. They were to
be married soon, and their friends planned, after the skating,
to go up to the house and present a gift to them. The gift and
the fact that the party was in her honour were to be a surprise
to Eunice. Nathan, for some reason, had been told about it.

There had been cold that year but no snow, so you could
skate all over the lake. My mother remembered them
skimming by, the golden lads and girls who made up the
world when she was small, and Nathan and Eunice the most
romantic of all. Nathan was handsome and Eunice was
beautiful and they were very much in love, she said.

She remembered the skaters by moonlight, slim black
shapes mysterious against the silver fields. There were a lot of
clouds in the sky that night and when the moon went behind
one of them, friends, neighbours and parents' friends became
alike: all equally unknown, unidentifiable.

My grandfather and Uncle Nathan had built a big wood fire
at the near end of the lake. My mother said that it was a grand
experience to skate off into the darkness and the perils and
dangers of the night, and then turn and come back toward the
light, following the fire's reflection on the ice.

Late on, when some people were already making their way
up the hill to the house, Eunice Lathem went skating off into
the darkness with her sister. They didn't skate up the middle
of the lake as most of the skaters had been doing. Instead they
went off toward the east bank. There is a place there where a
spring rises and the water is deep, but they didn't know that.
The ice was thinner there. They broke through.

Near the fire, people heard their cries for help. A group of
men skated out to rescue them. When the men got close to
the place where the girls were in the water, the ice began to
crack under their feet.

All the men lay down then and formed a chain, each
holding the ankles of the man in front of him. Uncle Nathan
was at the front. He inched forward, feeling the ice tremble
beneath his body, until he came to the point where he could

reach either of two pairs of hands clinging to the fractured edge.

It was dark. He couldn't see the girls' faces. All he could do was grasp the nearest pair of wrists and pull. The men behind him pulled on his feet. Together they dragged one girl back to safety. But as they were doing it, the ice broke away beneath them and the second girl went under. The moon came out and they saw it was Eunice Lathem's sister they had saved. They went back to the hole, but Eunice had vanished. There wasn't any way they could even get her body.

"It was an awful thing to have happen on our place," my father said.

"Your Uncle Nathan risked his life," my mother said. Her voice was earnest, for she too believed in identifying heroes and villains.

"There was no way on earth he could save both girls," she said. "The ice was already breaking, and the extra weight of the first one was bound to be too much for it."

Why hadn't he saved Eunice first?

"I told you," my mother said. "He couldn't see their faces."

It troubled me that he hadn't had some way of knowing. I would have expected love to be able to call out to love. If it couldn't do that, what was it good for? And why had the moon been behind a cloud anyway?

"Your grandmother used to say that the Lord moves in a mysterious way," my father said.

"What does that mean?" I asked.

"It means that nobody knows," my mother said.

I'd seen Eunice Lathem's name on a grave in the yard of St. Chad's, where we attended services every second Sunday. If I'd thought of her at all, it was as a person who had always been dead. Now she seemed real to me, almost like a relative. She was a girl who had loved and been loved. I began to make up stories about her. But I no longer skated on the lake alone.

Eunice Lathem's sister, whose name was Delia Sykes, moved away from Willow Bunch right after the accident. She didn't wait until her husband sold out; she went straight to Edmonton and waited for him there. Even when they buried Eunice in the spring, she didn't come back.

Years later, someone from Willow Bunch had seen her in Edmonton. She didn't mention Eunice or the accident or even Willow Bunch.

"It must have been a short conversation," my mother said practically.

Is it surprising that I continued to wonder why Uncle Nathan didn't marry? Some people remember their childhoods as a time when they thought of anybody over the age of 25 as being so decrepit as to be beyond all thought of romance or adventure. I remember feeling that way about *women*, but I never thought of men that way, whatever their ages. It seemed to me that Uncle Nathan could still pick out a girl and marry her if he set his mind to it.

"No," he said when I asked him. "Not 'still' and not 'pick out a girl.' A person doesn't have that much say in the matter. You can't love where you choose."

And then, making a joke of it, "See that you remember that when your time comes," he said.

One day my mother showed me a picture of Eunice Lathem and her sister. Two girls and a pony stood looking at the camera. Both girls were pretty. The one who wasn't Eunice was laughing; she looked like a girl who loved to laugh. Eunice was pretty too but there was a stillness about her, almost a sternness. If she hadn't been Eunice Lathem, I would have said she was sulking.

I felt cheated. Was the laughing one also prettier?

"She may have been," my mother said. "I remember Eunice Lathem as being beautiful. But since Delia Sykes was married, I don't suppose I gave her looks a thought one way or the other."

As I grew older I spent less time wondering about the girl who'd been Eunice Lathem. I'd never wondered about her sister, and perhaps never would have if I hadn't happened to be with Uncle Nathan the day he heard that Delia Sykes had died.

It was the spring I was fifteen. My parents were away for the weekend, attending a silver wedding in Rochfort Bridge. Uncle Nathan and I were alone on the farm and so, if he wanted to talk about Delia Sykes, he hadn't much choice about who to talk to.

It was a morning for bad news. The frost was coming out of the ground, setting the very ditches and wheel-ruts to weeping. Out in the barn, a ewe was mourning her lost lamb. We had put her in a pen by herself and we were saving the dead lamb, so we could use its skin to dress another lamb in case one of the ewes died in lambing or had no milk.

Uncle Nathan and I left the barn and walked out to the road to pick up the mail. The news of Delia's death was in the local paper. "Old-timers will be saddened to learn of the death in Duncan, B.C. of Mrs. Delia Sykes, a former resident of this district," the paper said.

Uncle Nathan shook his head slowly, as if he found the news hard to believe. "So Delia's gone," he said. "She was a grand girl, Delia Sykes. No matter what anybody said, she was a grand girl."

There was a picture of Mrs. Sykes with the death notice. I saw a middle-aged woman who had gone from the hair-dresser's to the photographer's. Her cheeks were as firm and round as two peach halves, and she had snappy eyes. She was wearing a white dress. She looked as if she might have belonged to the Eastern Star or the Rebekahs.

Uncle Nathan looked at the picture too. "Delia always was a beauty," he said.

He sat in silence for a while, and then, bit by bit, he began to tell me the story of how he had met Delia Sykes and before her, her husband.

"Only I didn't realize that he was her husband," Uncle Nathan said. "I thought when I met her that she was single; that was the joke of it."

It was late July and late afternoon. Uncle Nathan was teaching school, to make enough money to live on until his farm got going. But he was hoping to get out of it.

"The land was new then and we thought there was no limit to how rich we were all going to be some day. Besides that," he added, "what I wanted to do was farm. School-teaching seemed to me to be no proper job for a man."

There were two things Uncle Nathan wanted. One was to stop teaching. The other was to find a wife.

There were more men than girls around then, he told me, so the man who wanted a good selection had to be prepared to cover a lot of territory.

"Harold Knight and I took in dances and ball games as far away as Hasty Hills," he said.

They'd already seen a fair sampling, but there were still girls they hadn't seen.

"I had a pretty fair idea of what I was looking for," Uncle Nathan said. "I imagine it was the same sort of thing every young fellow thinks he's looking for, but I thought I had standards. I wasn't willing to settle for just anyone."

It was with the idea of looking over another couple of girls that he went to see Harold Knight that late July afternoon. A family with two daughters was rumoured to have moved in somewhere near Morningside School. He'd come to suggest to Harold that they take in the church service at the school the next Sunday.

The Knights, Uncle Nathan said, had hay and seed wheat to sell to people with the money to buy it. When Uncle Nathan walked into their yard that day, he saw that Mr. Knight was talking to a buyer. It was a man he'd never seen before, but he guessed by the cut of the man's rig that he must be well fixed.

"Nathan," Mr. Knight said, "meet Dobson Sykes."

Mr. Sykes was a straight-standing man with greying hair. He put out his hand and Uncle Nathan shook it.

"His driving horses," Uncle Nathan said, "were as showy a team as I'd ever seen — big bays with coats the colour of red willow."

"You'd go a long way before you'd find a better-matched team than that," Mr. Knight said.

"Oh, they match well enough." Dobson Sykes spoke as if that was a matter of little importance to him, as if no effort was made in the acquiring of such a team. "I'd trade them in a minute if something better came along," he said carelessly. "I have a job to keep Spark, here, up to his collar."

"I had a fair amount of respect then for men who'd done well in life," Uncle Nathan told me. "This man was about my father's age, old enough to have made it on his own. When a man like that came my way, I studied him. I thought if I was going to be a farmer instead of a teacher, I'd have to start figuring out how people went about getting things in life.

"I wasn't really surprised when Mr. Knight said that Sykes had a crew of men — men he was paying — putting up a set of buildings for him on a place he'd bought near Bannock Hill. He looked like a man with that kind of money."

"We're not building anything fancy," Dobson Sykes said. "If I'd wanted to stay farming on a big scale, I wouldn't have moved from Manitoba."

After a while Uncle Nathan left the two older men talking and walked out toward the meadow, where Harold was fetching a load of hay for Mr. Sykes.

It was on the trail between buildings and meadow that he met Delia Sykes.

He didn't see her at first because she wasn't sitting up front with Harold. She must have been lying back in the hay, Uncle Nathan said, just watching the clouds drift by overhead. She sat up.

Uncle Nathan saw at once that she was not very old; he had girls almost as old as she was in his classroom. But there was nothing of the schoolgirl about Delia. She was young but womanly. Everything about her curved, from the line of her cheek to the way she carried her arms.

Uncle Nathan saw all this in the instant that she appeared looking down over the edge of the load. He saw too that she had a kind of class he'd never seen around Willow Bunch. She looked like a girl perfectly suited to riding around the country behind a team of perfectly matched bays.

She reached behind her into the hay and came up with a crown of french-braided dandelions. She set it on top of her hair and smiled.

He knew right then, Uncle Nathan said, that his voice wouldn't be among those swelling the hymns at Morningside School next Sunday. And he felt as if he understood for the first time how men must feel when they are called to the ministry. Choosing and decision and standards have nothing to do with it. You're called or you're not called, and when you're called you know it.

The girl smiled and opened her arms as if to take in the clouds in the sky and the bees buzzing in the air and the red-topped grasses stirring in the wind. Then she spoke.

"You've got no worries on a load of hay," she said.

Those were the first words Uncle Nathan heard Delia Sykes say. "You've got no worries on a load of hay."

There was a patch of milkweed blooming near the path where Uncle Nathan was standing. In late July, small pink blossoms appear and the milk, rich and white, is ready to run as soon as you break the stalk. Uncle Nathan picked a branch, climbed the load of hay, and presented it to the girl.

"It's not roses," he said, "but the sap is supposed to cure warts."

She laughed. "My name is Delia Sykes," she said.

"I thought she was Dobson's daughter," Uncle Nathan said, "and it crossed my mind to wonder if he'd have traded her off if she hadn't moved along smart in her harness.

"There didn't seem to be much fear of that. You could see right away she had spirit. If she had too much, it was nothing that marriage to a good man wouldn't cure, I thought."

Uncle Nathan gave a rueful smile. "Of course when we got back to the yard I found out that she wasn't Dobson's daughter but his wife. Later I wonder why she hadn't introduced herself as *Mrs.* Sykes. And she'd called me *Nathan* too, and girls didn't do that then.

"The truth is," Uncle Nathan said, "I had kind of fallen for her."

Did she feel the same way about him?

If she did, Uncle Nathan wasn't willing to say so. "Delia was only nineteen," he said. "I don't think she knew what she wanted."

He was silent for a while. Then he went on with his story. "Once I knew she was married," he said, "I knew right away what I had to do. I remember I gave myself a good talking to. I said, 'If you can fall in love in twenty minutes, you can fall out of love just as fast.'"

"And could you?"

"Some people could, I guess," Uncle Nathan said. "It seemed to take me a bit longer than that."

The story stopped then because we had to go out to the barn to check the sheep. While we'd been in the house, another ewe had dropped her lamb. We heard it bleat as we came in the barn, and the ewe whose lamb had died heard it too. It was at the far end of the barn, out of sight, but at the sound of it, milk began to run from her udder. She couldn't help herself.

We checked the rest of the sheep and then we went back into the house. I made us a pot of tea.

"I was afraid to go to see Dobson and Delia after they got moved in," Uncle Nathan said. "I think I was afraid somebody would read my mind."

He went, he said, because Delia soon made her house a gathering place for all the young people of the district, and he didn't see how he could be the only one to stay away. Delia didn't make things any easier for him.

"She used to keep saying she'd only been married three months ... as if that made it any less final. And when she spoke of anything they had — whether it was a buggy or a kitchen safe or the pet dog — she would say 'my buggy' or 'my kitchen safe' or 'my dog.' 'We' and 'us' were words she didn't use at all."

I poured our tea then, trying to imagine the house that Delia Sykes had lived in.

"It was something of a showplace for its time," Uncle Nathan told me. Everything in it was the best of its kind, he said, from the Home Comfort stove in the kitchen to the pump organ in the parlour. What puzzled Uncle Nathan was Delia's attitude to her things. She'd picked them out herself in Winnipeg and ordered them sent, but when they got here, she seemed to feel they weren't important.

"The more things you've got, the more things you've got to take care of," she said. She didn't even unpack most of her trunks.

Dobson was worried. He thought that moving away from her family had unsettled her. "Delia wasn't like this in Manitoba," he said.

"I kept wondering," Uncle Nathan said, "where we would go from here. It never occurred to me that there could be another girl for me. And then Eunice came along."

It was on an October afternoon, Uncle Nathan said, that he met Eunice Lathem.

The sun was low in the southwest when he drove into the Sykes yard, and Dobson, as usual, was out around the buildings showing the younger men his grinding mill, his blacksmith shop, his threshing machine.

Uncle Nathan remembered that the trees were leafless except for the plumes of new growth at the top. He tied up his horse and, as he headed for the house, saw that the afternoon sun was turning the west-facing walls all gold and blue. It looked like a day for endings, not beginnings. But he went into the house, and there stood Eunice Lathem.

Eunice was a year or two older than Delia but she looked just like her. Uncle Nathan noticed that she was quieter.

Supper was already on the table when Uncle Nathan got there. The news of Eunice's arrival had attracted such a company of bachelors that there weren't enough plates or chairs for everybody to eat at once.

"I don't know about anybody else, but I'm starving," Delia announced, taking her place at the head of the table. Eunice, though she was the guest of honour, insisted on waiting until the second sitting.

As the first eaters prepared to deal with their pie, Eunice began to ladle water out of a stonewear crock into a dishpan. Uncle Nathan went to help her. He said something funny and she laughed.

Delia's voice startled them both. "I invited Eunice out here to find a husband," she said with a high-pitched laugh. "I said to myself, 'With all the bachelors we've got around, if she can't find a husband here, there's no hope for her.'"

Delia spoke as if she was making a joke, and there was a nervous round of laughter. Blood rose in Eunice's face.

"If I'd known that was why you were asking me," Eunice said, "I would never have come."

And indeed, Uncle Nathan said, Eunice wasn't the sort of girl to need anyone's help in finding a husband. She was, if anything, prettier than Delia. Not as showy, perhaps, perhaps not as rounded. But if you went over them point by point comparing noses, chins, teeth and all the rest of it, Eunice might well have come out on top.

Later, when the others had gone, Delia apologized. "I shouldn't have said that," she said. "It sounded awful." She didn't even claim to have been making a joke.

"I want you two to be friends," she said.

In the weeks that followed, Uncle Nathan saw that Delia was pushing her sister his way. He didn't know why, but he didn't find the idea unpleasant.

"I suppose I liked Eunice at first because she looked so

much like Delia," he said, "but as I got to know her better it seemed to me that she might be easier to get along with in the long run. I wouldn't be the first man to marry the sister of the girl who first took his fancy, nor the last one either.

"It seemed to me that a man could love one girl as easily as another if he put his mind to it. I reasoned it out. How much did the person matter anyway? That was what I asked myself. It seemed to me that when all was said and done, it would be the life that two people made together that would count, not who the people were.

"I remember thinking that getting married would be like learning to dance. Some people are born knowing how; they have a natural beat. Other people have to make an effort to learn. But all of them, finally, are moving along to the music one way or the other.

"Anyway," Uncle Nathan said, "I spoke to Eunice, and she agreed, and we decided to be married at Christmas.

"It was September, I think, when we got engaged," Uncle Nathan said. "I remember thinking about telling Dobson and Delia. I could imagine the four of us — Dobson and Delia, Eunice and me — living side by side, spending our Sundays together, raising children who would be cousins and might even look like each other.

"I came over early on the Sunday and we told them. Delia didn't have very much to say then. But in the afternoon when quite a crowd had gathered and Eunice and I were waiting for the rest of them to get there before we made our announcement, a strange thing happened.

"The day before, Dobson had brought home a new saddle pony and Delia had wanted to ride it. Dobson didn't know how well broke it was, or if it could be trusted, and he refused. I guess that refusal rankled. Delia didn't like to be told she couldn't do a thing or have a thing she had set her heart on.

"Anyway, on Sunday afternoon Eunice was sitting at the pump organ playing for us, and she looked beautiful. We were all sitting around looking at her.

"And then somebody happened to glance out of the window," Uncle Nathan said. "And there was Delia on the pony and the pair of them putting on a regular rodeo.

"She didn't break her neck, which was a wonder. By the time she finally got off the pony, we were all out in the yard, and somebody had the idea of taking a picture of Delia and Eunice and the pony."

After that, Uncle Nathan said, Delia seemed to want to get the wedding over with as soon as possible. She hemmed sheets and ordered linen and initialled pillow-cases. When November finally came and the neighbours decided on a skating party for Eunice and Uncle Nathan, it was Delia who sewed white rabbit fur around the sleeves and bottom of Eunice's coat, so that it would look like a skating dress.

The night of the party was dark. There was a moon, but the sky was cloudy. They walked down the hill together, all those young people, laughing and talking.

"One minute you could see their faces and the next they would all disappear," Uncle Nathan said. "I touched a match to a bonfire we had laid in the afternoon, and we all sat down to screw on our skates.

"I skated first with Eunice. She wanted to stay near the fire so we could see where we were going. I skated with several other girls, putting off, for some reason, the time when I would skate with Delia. But then she came gliding up to me and held out her hands, and I took them and we headed out together into the darkness.

"As soon as we turned our backs on the fire it was as if something came over us. We wanted to skate out farther and farther. It seemed to me that we could keep on like this all our lives, just skating outward farther and farther, and the lake would keep getting longer and longer so that we would never come to the end of it."

Uncle Nathan sighed. "I didn't know then that in three days Delia would have left Willow Bunch for good, and in six months I would have followed her," he said.

Why had he given up farming?

"Farming's no life for a man alone," he said. "And I couldn't imagine ever wanting to marry again."

He resumed his story. "Once the moon came out and I could see Delia's face, determined in the moonlight.

" 'Do you want to turn back?' I asked her.

" 'I'm game as long as you are,' she said.

"Another time, 'I don't ever want to turn back,' she said.

"I gave in before Delia did," Uncle Nathan said. " 'If we don't turn around pretty soon,' I told her, 'we're going to be skating straight up Pa's stubble fields.'

"We turned around then, and there was the light from the fire and our feet already set on its path. And I found I wanted to be back there with all the people around me. Eunice deserved better, and I knew it."

As they came toward the fire, Eunice skated out to meet them. "I might as well have been someplace else for all the attention she paid me," Uncle Nathan said. Her words were all for Delia.

"If this is what you got me out here for," Eunice said, "you can just forget about it. I'm not going to be your window blind."

"I don't know what you're talking about," Delia said.

She looked unhappy. "She knew as well as I did," Uncle Nathan said, "that whatever we were doing out there, it was more than just skating."

"We were only skating," Delia said. And then her temper rose. "You always were jealous of me," she said.

"Who would you say was jealous now?" Eunice asked.

"We were far enough away from the fire for the girls not to be heard," Uncle Nathan said. "At least I hoped we were.

"What was worrying me was the thought of Eunice having to meet all the people up at the house, and finding out she was the guest of honour, and having to try to rise to the occasion.

"That was why I suggested that the two of them go for a skate. I thought it would give them a chance to cool down.

Besides," he added, "I couldn't think of anything else to do."

The girls let themselves be persuaded. They skated off together and Uncle Nathan watched them go. First he could see their two silhouettes, slim and graceful against the silver lake. Then all he could see was the white fur on Eunice's coat. And then they were swallowed up by the darkness.

"It was several minutes before we heard them calling for help," Uncle Nathan said.

Uncle Nathan and I sat silent for some time then: he remembering, I pondering. "If only you could have seen how beautiful she was," he said at last, and I didn't know whether it was Eunice he was speaking of, or Delia.

"I wonder if I would have felt any better about it if I'd got Eunice instead of Delia," he said. I realized that he'd been trying to make the judgment for 30 years.

"You didn't have any choice," I reminded him. "It was dark. You couldn't see their faces."

"No," Uncle Nathan said. "I couldn't see their faces." The sound of old winters was in his voice, a sound of infinite sadness.

"But I could see their hands on the edge of the ice," he said. "The one pair of arms had white fur around them.

"And I reached for the other pair."

The Hanged Man

In my country, when someone kills his neighbour they hang him. It's stupid, but that's the way it is. It's in the laws.

My job is to watch over the hanged. In the prison where I work, a hanged man isn't taken down as soon as he is dead. No, he is left hanging all night and it's my job to watch over him until sunrise.

I'm not required to weep, but I do weep all the same.

I knew very well this hanged man wasn't going to be an ordinary hanged man. Unlike all the condemned men I had seen up to then, this one didn't seem to be afraid. He didn't smile, but his eyes didn't betray any fear. He looked at the gallows coldly, whereas the other condemned men almost unfailingly go into shock when they see it. Yes, I felt that this hanged man wouldn't be an ordinary hanged man.

When the trapdoor opened and the rope stretched taut with a dry sound, I felt something move in my belly.

The hanged man didn't struggle. All those I had seen till this one had twisted

MICHEL
TREMBLAY

about, swinging at the end of the rope with their knees drawn up. But this one didn't move.

He didn't die immediately. You could hear him trying to breathe. . . . But he didn't move. He didn't move at all. We looked at each other, the hangman, the prison governor and I, wrinkling our foreheads. This lasted a few minutes; then, suddenly, the hanged man let out a long yell that sounded to me like the huge laughter of a madman. The hangman said that was the end.

The hanged man quivered. His body seemed to lengthen a little. Then, nothing more.

But I was sure he had laughed.

I was alone with the hanged man who had laughed. I couldn't stop myself from looking at him. He seemed to have grown longer still. And that hood I have always hated! That hood which hides everything but lets you imagine everything! I never see the faces of the hanged, but I guess what they're like and I think that's even worse.

All the lights had been put out and the little nightlight over the door had been lit.

How black it was and how afraid I was of this hanged man.

In spite of myself, around two in the morning, I dozed off. I was woken — I couldn't say just when — by a low sound, like a sigh. Was it me who had sighed like that? It must have been me, I was alone. I had probably sighed in my sleep and my sigh had woken me.

Instinctively, I turned my eyes towards the hanged man. He had moved! He had made a quarter turn and now he was facing me. It wasn't the first time this had happened. It was due to the rope, I knew that perfectly well. But all the same I couldn't help trembling. And that sigh. That sigh which I wasn't certain had come out of my mouth.

I called myself a double-dyed idiot and got up to walk around a bit. As soon as I had turned my back on the hanged man, I heard the sigh again. I was quite sure this time that it wasn't me who had sighed. I didn't dare turn around. I felt my legs turn to water and my throat dry up. I heard two or three more sighs, which soon changed into breathing, first very uneven, then more regular. I was absolutely certain the hanged man was breathing and I thought I was going to faint.

At last I turned round, trembling all over. The dead man was moving. He was swinging, almost imperceptibly, at the end of his rope. And he was breathing more and more strongly. I got as far away from him as I could, taking refuge in a corner of the big room.

I shall never forget the horrible spectacle that followed. The hanged man had been breathing for about five minutes, when he started to laugh. He suddenly stopped breathing loudly and began to laugh softly. It wasn't a demoniacal, or even a cynical, laugh; it was simply the laugh of someone who is wildly amused. His laughter quickly grew louder and soon the hanged man was roaring with laughter, fit to burst his sides. He was swinging more and more violently . . . laughing . . . laughing . . .

I was sitting on the ground, my two arms squeezed to my stomach, and I was crying.

The dead man was swinging so violently that at one moment his feet almost touched the ceiling. This went on for several minutes. Minutes of pure terror for me. Suddenly the rope broke and I let out a loud cry. The hanged man hit the ground with a thud. His head came off and rolled over to my feet. I jumped up and ran for the door.

When the caretaker, the prison governor and I returned to the room, the body was still there, stretched out in a corner; but we couldn't find the dead man's head. It was never found.

Tudor King

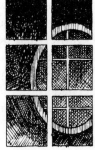"Will he be all right?" the boy asked again. Against the cold his breathing came in short gasps and his normally round face was pinched together expectantly to the huge parka-ed figure beside him.

"I told you — we'll see when we get there," his brother Frank flipped the reins gently against the flanks of the horses. Encouraged, they butted their way into another drift driven behind the brush skirting the road. "Don't talk. Just stop wriggling, keep the robe up — tight."

Immediately the boy settled back and resolved again not to make another move until they got there. The question, however, ran on through his mind in circular repetition, like Little Black Sambo's tigers around and around the tree. Remembering that naked little fellow, the boy involuntarily hunched lower into the blankets for warmth, eyes squinting at the storm-wasted world. His father had said it had been the worst storm to ever hit the district. For five days the blizzard had whipped the pellet-snow across the land; one evening only the ropes they

RUDY
WIEBE

had strung between house and barn had brought Frank safely in from feeding the stock. But last night when the boy awoke there had been no storm whine. What he heard as he lay, limp from sleep and staring at the red bulge of the heater, was the sad howl of the wolves, hunger-desperate after the storm. He had heard, and felt something finger down his spine even as he curled up more tightly, pulling the wool quilt up and over, and then he had heard his father just beyond the bedroom partition make a sound in his sleep and the long moans had lost their hold and he had lain snug, his eyes wide again to the cheery heater. Abruptly he had remembered the old man, thought of all the after-blizzard nights he must have lain in his sagging cabin, hearing the wolves. With no father to clear his throat in the darkness.

Now, the team plowing steadily ahead, the boy shuddered again. He sensed Frank looking at him and to cover up he rubbed his nose fast with the back of his mitten. Somehow that did not seem enough: he crouched lower in the seat of the cutter and lifted the heavy robe over his head. The musty smell of the cow-hide brought him back to the old man again because that was his cabin smell too. Mixed with some others.

His father had said the old man was already there when they came to their homestead. Probably he had always lived there, bent, scum-grey hair projecting from his face and under his cap, pants held up by twine, stitched together with string, old. On warmer days in spring and summer he shuffled past their farm every week towards the store which was also post office, his hands folded behind his back, a greyish sack held in place by cord over his shoulder. And at his heels followed the dog, small, brownish, and always bald at varying spots from his truceless battle with fleas. Like the other children of the settlement, the boy stared at the stooped figure almost apprehensively from behind a tree or barn-corner. The name, hissed at bedtime, was enough to quiet any restless youngster.

But once, last summer, the boy had faced him. On a long Sunday afternoon the boy and two friends, daring each other into a corner beyond their courage, had inched up to the cabin where the old man lived. Someone, with gritted teeth, knocked. And then the door squeaked open and they were inside where the litter, gathered home over years in the greyish sack, left them barely room to shuffle their feet. The dog, squatting on the sack-heaped bedstead too, looked more miserable than ever, but something had happened to the old man. In the darkness under the robe the boy, now as then, saw him in awe. And heard his voice.

"Think I'm in bad shape, huh? You," jabbing a finger at the tallest of the three, "you taken history?" He said it as if there were only one bit of history to be known and it could be taken like a pill.

Henry nodded hastily.

"It says the Tudors was once kings of England. Eh!" The last was not a question; his whole body jerked as he shot it out.

Henry, whose head was still bobbing slightly from the previous question, said quickly, "Uh-huh!" because that was one bit he did seem to know.

"Well, what's my name?" The boys could say nothing, quite floundered that the old man should ask such a thing. Even the dog had stopped scratching. "Eh!"

Henry ventured, very gently, "Mr — Tudor."

"Eh!" The ejaculation snapped at them like a whip: in the gathering wonder of that moment the three suddenly comprehended. Under the robe, the boy could again see the flash of the grey eyes and again he was mesmerized. "That means I come from them same Tudors that was kings of England. You know what that means?" The voice, not creaking now but great, "I'm a Tudor. I should be king of England."

As if suddenly aware of their numb comprehension, the old man relented a little, but the flame in his eye did not die. "Now I ain't saying I'm against the King. I ain't really, no, only I don't think he's running the war right. Look at what that Hitler's doing to the people. Even bombing them! I ain't against him, but if George was to come out from England and say, 'Tudor, will you take over?' why, I wouldn't refuse him. Eh!''

As on that summer day, the boy heard no more of the voice but in the musty, seeping coldness under the robe he again saw the old man before him. And the dingy flesh obvious through the rags, the bedraggled whiskers, the rotting shoes, even the dog with his ceaseless scratch, were transformed. If before him was the nadir of humanity, the flashing eyes and the compulsive spirit moving there revealed the stuff of majesty. The lined face was no longer directed toward the palpable ambitions of youth; no longer toward an actuality or even a probability. Whatever had crushed any fulfillable ambition had not been able to erase a fragment of history, or prevent it from blossoming in the failing mind of the old man.

The boy had not actually known this on the last summer afternoon as he and his friends stood dumb in the cabin. He did not even know it now under the robe on his way to see how the old man had weathered the storm: if asked directly, he could have shaped no words to explain himself. He simply knew what he had seen in the wreck before him, and the two miles home had vanished under his feet as he sped to tell all he could put in words: I saw a king! And the disappointment struck him again as he remembered how Frank had laughed.

"Ah Andy. That's his dream. Told me years ago. Dream — what else can he do, now?"

He stood sullen in the warm dust of the barnyard. The Tudors *had* been kings of England; it was in a book at school. And the old man's name *was* Tudor. So he must be from the same family, and so the throne belonged as much to him as King George VI. And the way he had looked and the way he had spoken —

Frank put down the book he was reading and leaned back against the haystack. "Sorry Andy, I didn't think you really believed him." He looked over the trees into the sky and added slowly, "But you're almost ten. You've got to learn sometime that you can't believe everything. It's okay to dream about chasing wolves and flying planes — every boy does — but you can't go around believing every old tramp that says he's a king. Even if his name happens to fit something, four hundred years ago."

Seeing the boy stare wordlessly at the ground, he insisted, "Kid, you can tell. He's not really right anymore, up here. He's lived alone and with that dog too long. A man can become low and cheap if he just lives with himself too long. He can become no man at all. How can a man live as he does — in a shack full of junk and that filthy runt. That's what you saw. Listen. Just last week Ted Martin was missing some eggs again. He had a good idea where they were going, so when he met old Tudor on the road he said, 'You know, I've been losing eggs out of my barn again.'

" 'Oh,' says old Tudor, 'Say, there must be a snitcher around. Just yesterday I was missing some — '

" 'Yah,' Ted interrupted, 'but I'm fixing him. I'll plant some poisoned eggs in that barn and we'll see what's what.'

"Ted said Tudor's eyes got all big and scared, 'Hey Ted, you wouldn't do a thing like that to an old friend, would you?' "

After a moment Frank said heavily, "All these years he's lived alone, in dirt. Too long. All the truth and pride in him — everything's rotten away. What can you believe him?"

But no logic or facts could budge the idea caught in the gleam of the old man's eye as he sat enthroned among the sacks of his bed. The boy could no more deny it than he could understand it. But it was there.

He heard Frank shout "Haw!" and he felt the cutter lurch to the left. He thrust his head above the robe; they were turning off the main road up the drifted track to the cabin now, the greys steaming, heaving themselves forward together. The jack-pine and scrawny outline poplars crowded closer here. It was too cold for wind or even clouds: there was just one massive inhuman concentration on cold. The sunlight blazing on the drift-driven snow only added ironical emphasis.

But the cold, sting as it might, could not hold his thoughts. *Around the copse and then we'll see*, he thought, keeping even the cold at arm's length. *Just around the corner. A few more steps that one more big drift, and there it will be —*

Only it was not. When they rounded the last pine they saw no cabin in the clearing. The boy jerked to his feet. Where the cabin should have been hunched in the lee of a small hill there was only the straight waste of a giant drift that had levelled the clearing to lose itself at the edge of the spruce. Then, his eyes skipping back over the drift, he saw the bit of stove-pipe sticking up and he knew that the wind had only buried the shack and that beneath the hard surface it was snug and — then he looked at the stove-pipe again.

"Frank," he said.

His brother was standing too, huge, his weathered face rimmed by the frost on his parka. "Yah," he said.

The horses fought their way a bit closer, then halted at a word. Frank muttered, "Hang on here," giving the boy the reins, and stepped out to pull the blankets over the hot horses. "I agreed to watch him, but the Mounties can't blame me. Not for a five day blizzard."

"Frank —"

"Stay in the cutter! Get under there and stay warm. Y'hear!" The boy, knowing his brother was rough because he had just said what he need not have said, and yet having been compelled to say it though useless, sat down slowly and watched him bull himself into the deepening snow. From this angle the boy could see that the wind had eddied the snow clear within a few feet of one side of the cabin, leaving a curving rift in the drift. He saw the iceless glass of one small window: he looked at the stove-pipe. No smoke. He remembered the look of the old man. He dropped the reins and was out, his legs churning along the straggled trail. Frank wheeled at him, mouth open to thunder, then after an instant stooped without a word to continue clearing the door.

The inner door ground a cracking protest on its leather hinges. Beyond the flash of snow the interior was black as Frank pushed back his hood and stepped in. He completely blocked the opening, but the boy, hunching over, slipped past his legs. As he stood there facing the gloom he could feel the old trunk against his leg and he knew from the shadows that the clutter of pottery and worn-out harness of the summer before was still upon it. Through a corner of the east window the sunlight now managed a faint reflection, outlining in ragged silhouette the heaps of things crowding the room. The stove-pipe stood above the hump of the heater against the middle of the low ceiling. The boy's mittened hand reached up to the edge of Frank's parka in the silence of their breathing.

"Uh — Tudor," Frank cleared his throat gruffly. Then more loudly, "Tudor, you here?" His voice bounced about.

After a moment Frank started into the room. "He saw a hundred storms — had enough wood for four days if he skimped." He leaned forward in the gloom about the heater. "Maybe he tried to go out for more — there's none h — Oh."

He straightened instantly, brushing away the boy's hand. "Andy, you better get back to the cutter, and . . ." but there was no need to finish. More accustomed to the half-light, the boy had already seen the figure curled tight against the heater, the back cramped against it as though to plead some touch of warmth from its rigid flank. They both leaned closer as sunlight from the door fell on the granite face. An icicle of saliva had frozen the mouth and beard to the floor.

Frank said, "Wonder, where's the dog."

The boy, still gripping the parka, pointed.

"Huh?" Frank's glance moved slowly around the room, ending on the bed bare to its rope springs. His hands fumbled slightly as he thrust his mitts more firmly onto them, then, with an abrupt movement he bent down. Rigidly, as a welded iron framework, the whole shape moved. He half-straightened and said strangely. "No weight to it." Then quickly he reached in and pulled the dog from where it had been cradled, hugged, in the nest of rags. It seemed at that moment to be turning stiff. Even as Frank pushed something aside and eased it to the floor, the hairless limbs stretched rigid also.

Frank said slowly, "He tried his best for the dog. Knowing we'd come when the storm dropped, Old Man Tudor."

Then he suddenly turned. The boy felt himself lifted up in his brother's strong arms, held close as he had not been since he was a small child. But he did not find that strange. Something was breaking through his numbness, painful and wet, and he pushed his face against his brother's hard, cold shoulder; as if he were already remembering his own fierce happiness at once having recognized the fleeting stuff of human majesty.

Biographical and Critical Notes on Individual Authors

COLLEEN ARCHER

Colleen Archer was born in Winnipeg, Manitoba and is presently (1984) living in Omemee, Ontario where she writes and looks after her cats, dogs, horses, and children. She studied at Carleton University and at the University of Manitoba. Although she devotes most of her time now to fiction writing, Archer has been a tax consultant, a secretary, a news correspondent, and an instructor for the YWCA. She is married and has two daughters.

In addition to writing fiction for children and adults, Archer writes poems and articles for magazines both here and in the United States. Her love of animals and her concern about the abuse of animals are reflected not only in the story "The Dog Who Wanted to Die" (winner of the 1983 **Vicky Metcalf Award**) but also in her poetry and articles.

JOYCE BARKHOUSE

Joyce Barkhouse was born in Annapolis Valley, Nova Scotia. She attended Nova Scotia Teachers' College and taught elementary school for several years in that province as well as in Quebec. She has two children and five grandchildren.

Barkhouse has won several awards for her writing which, in addition to short stories and articles, includes book-length biographies of George Dawson and Abraham Gesner. Along with Margaret Atwood, she produced the well-known children's book, *Anna's Pet*. In 1982 Barkhouse received the **Cultural Life Award of the Province of Nova Scotia**. Many of Barkhouse's stories and books are set in Nova Scotia.

MORLEY CALLAGHAN

Morley Callaghan was born in Toronto, Ontario and educated at the University of Toronto before studying law at Osgoode Hall. Although he has done a lot of travelling—most memorably, perhaps, to Paris where he and Ernest Hemingway were friends—he has spent most of his life in Ontario. Callaghan was a reporter with the *Toronto Star* and later worked with the Royal Canadian Navy on assignment for the NFB.

Author of numerous novels, plays, and short stories, Callaghan has been the recipient of many awards, among them the **Governor-General's Award** in 1952 and the **Royal Bank of Canada Award** for $50 000 in 1970. Callaghan's works explore the psychological complexities of human relationships, frequently stressing the importance of loyalty and honesty and the misery associated with a guilty conscience. While Callaghan writes what might be called moral tales, he is careful not to moralize.

HUGH GARNER

Hugh Garner was born in Yorkshire, England but moved to Canada with his family when he was six. He grew up in "Cabbagetown", then a poor section of Toronto. It has served as the locale for many of his stories and novels. He has held numerous jobs, among them copy boy for the *Toronto Star*, wheat stooker in Saskatchewan, and freelance journalist. He also served with the Canadian Navy during World War II.

Garner has tremendous sympathy for outsiders and losers. Although he portrays his characters with all of their flaws, he somehow manages to enlist the reader's sympathy on their behalf. His last novel, *Murder Has Your Number*, was published in 1978, a year before his death. Garner received the **Governor-General's Award** in 1963 for his short stories.

ELIZABETH KAUFMAN

Elizabeth Kaufman was born in Halifax, Nova Scotia and has also lived in Toronto, Muskoka, and Kitchener for short periods. Her present (1984) home is in the St. George area near Cambridge, Ontario and is situated on a beautiful, treed, two-hectare property. She attended schools in the United States for a short time and also in Toronto where she studied Business Education.

Although she has won the **Dorothy Shoemaker Literary Award**, her duties as librarian in South Dumfries and her interests in animals, crafts, young people, books, and music leave her little time for writing. Her stories reflect her interest in young people and her love of nature.

W.P. KINSELLA

W.P. Kinsella was born in Edmonton, Alberta and presently (1984) divides his time between Edmonton, White Rock, B.C., and Iowa City, Iowa. He received his B.A. from the University of Victoria and his Masters of Fine Art from the University of Iowa. Although he devotes most of his time to writing (and to watching baseball games), he has been an Insurance Investigator, a salesperson, a taxi driver, a university professor, and, he claims, "a viking". In 1983 he wrote and narrated for the CBC a series of unforgettable vignettes about the traditions, characters, and legends associated with the world of baseball.

In addition to his award-winning novel, *Shoeless Joe*, Kinsella has won popular and critical acclaim for his numerous short stories, his outspoken articles and reviews, and his books on baseball. He is perhaps best known for his ability to take readers into unfamiliar worlds and make them feel at home there.

FARLEY MOWAT

Farley Mowat was born in Belleville, Ontario and educated at the University of Toronto. He is presently (1984) living in Cape Breton, Nova Scotia. As a young man he spent several years as a soldier and two very influential years in the Arctic, years that have had a profound effect on almost everything he has written.

Mowat's greatest concern is for "the fate of animate creation—human and non-human". While his books have helped to bring the plight of the Inuit and Newfoundland Outporters to the attention of the government, the results of government intervention have not always been to his liking, nor to the liking of some Newfoundlanders. Mowat has won numerous awards, among them the **Governor-General's Award** for *Lost in the Barrens* (*Two Against the North*) in 1965 and the **Stephen Leacock Medal** for humour for *The Boat that Wouldn't Float* in 1968.

ALICE MUNRO

Alice Munro was born and brought up in Wingham, Ontario, a small town near Lake Huron. She studied at the University of Western Ontario in London, and later moved to Vancouver, British Columbia. She has three children and is presently (1984) living in Clinton, Ontario. Her first volume of short stories, *Dance of the Happy Shades*, won the **Governor-General's Award** for fiction when it was published in 1968. She has, since then, won many other awards and international recognition. She won the **Governor-General's Award** again in 1978 for *Who Do You Think You Are?*

Munro's stories are subtle, honest, and deeply human. Very often they explore the worlds of those who do not fully understand their worlds themselves. She shows particular concern for the young, the poor, the old, the uneducated, the inarticulate, and those who are not at ease socially.

ALDEN NOWLAN

Alden Nowlan was born in Stanley, a rural area near Windsor, Nova Scotia. In his late teens he moved to Hartland, New Brunswick where he became reporter and later news editor for the local paper. From 1963-1968 he was night news editor for *The Telegraph Journal*, a Saint John publication. He spent most of the last fifteen years of his life in Fredericton where he was writer-in-residence at the University of New Brunswick. He has not only written articles for all of Canada's leading magazines, but has published more than ten volumes of poetry, numerous short stories, a novel, and several plays. In 1967 he received the **Governor-General's Award** for *Bread, Wine, and Salt*. When he died in 1983, he left a wife and one son.

Although Nowlan has tried almost every kind of writing at one time or another—and succeeded at all of them—he is, first and foremost, a poet. His language is direct, his style uncluttered, and his knowledge of the subtle workings of the human soul, profound.

GERALDINE RUBIA

Geraldine Rubia has spent most of her life in the towns and cities on the Avalon Peninsula in Newfoundland. She is presently (1984) living in Mount Pearl near St. John's. She graduated from high school while a patient in the orthopaedic wing of the General Hospital in St. John's. Since then she has taken university courses in Speech and Drama, Journalism, and Creative Writing. She is married and has two sons.

Rubia has been a rehabilitation counsellor for the disabled for many years and since 1981 has been the Assistant Director for the Newfoundland Rehabilitation Services. In 1968 she was named Handicapped Woman of the Year. Rubia has won awards not only for her short stories, but also for her poetry and plays. She loves writing, gardening, music, reading, and roaming the rugged Newfoundland seashore.

MERNA SUMMERS

Merna Summers was born in Mannville, Alberta and is presently (1984) living in Edmonton, Alberta. She was a reporter for the *Edmonton Journal* for eight years but now devotes most of her time to writing novels and stories. In addition to writing, Summers enjoys speaking Spanish and reading Latin American literature. She has won several awards for her writing, among them the **Katherine Anne Porter Award** for short fiction.

Most of the stories in Summers' two volumes of stories, *The Skating Party* and *Calling Home*, are set in the fictional town of Willow Bunch. Readers believe in this town and in its inhabitants because of Summers' ability to imbue the particular and the regional with the light of universal truth.

MICHEL TREMBLAY

Michel Tremblay was born in Montreal, Quebec and still makes his home in that province. He was a linotype operator for a short time but decided to devote his energies to writing. One of Canada's best known playwrights, Tremblay has more than a dozen plays to his credit, many of which have been translated into other languages. Translations of his plays have been produced in Great Britain, Italy, Japan, and New Zealand, as well as in English-speaking Canada and in the United States.

In addition to writing plays, Tremblay writes very successful novels, some of which he has read on CBC radio's *Booktime* series. In his plays and novels, Tremblay juxtaposes the familiar and the bizarre, the conventional and the eccentric, in ways that make his characters unforgettable. Most of his short stories, like "The Hanged Man", focus on Gothic and/or surreal situations.

RUDY WIEBE

Rudy Wiebe was born near Fairholme, Saskatchewan and moved to Coaldale, Alberta when he was twelve. He attended universities in Manitoba and Alberta and also in West Germany. He is presently (1984) teaching at the University of Alberta in Edmonton. He and his wife have three children. He is the author of several novels and two books of short stories as well as numerous television dramas and documentaries.

Wiebe's parents were Mennonite farmers who came to Canada from Russia before their son was born. This Mennonite background has shaped Wiebe's belief in social responsibility, moral strength, and passivism. His love for language and his basic respect for all human beings regardless of colour, creed, or social class are reflected in everything he writes. Although his novels and stories are usually set in the Prairies, they speak to human beings everywhere.

Policy Statement

Prentice-Hall Canada Inc., Educational Book Division, and the editor of *Windows and Mirrors* are committed to the publication of instructional materials that are as bias-free as possible. This anthology was evaluated for bias prior to publication.

The editor and publisher also recognize the importance of appropriate reading levels and have therefore made every effort to ensure the highest degree of readability in the student text. The content has been selected, organized, and written at a level suitable to the intended audience. Standard readability tests have been applied to ensure an appropriate reading level.

Research indicates, however, that readability is affected by much more than word or sentence length; factors such as presentation, format and design, none of which are considered in the usual readability tests, also greatly influence the ease with which students read a book. These and many additional features have been carefully prepared to ensure maximum student comprehension.

Acknowledgments

"The Dog Who Wanted to Die" by Colleen Archer: reprinted by permission of the author.

"The Heroine of Lunenburg" by Joyce Barkhouse: first published in *The Dancing Sun*, Press Porcepic Limited, Victoria, B.C., 1981. Reprinted by permission of the author.

"Very Special Shoes" by Morley Callaghan: reprinted by permission of Macmillan of Canada, A Division of Canada Publishing Corporation.

"The Father" by Hugh Garner: reprinted by permission of McGraw-Hill Ryerson Limited.

"Grandfather's Special Magic" by Elizabeth Kaufman: from *The Dancing Sun*, edited by Jan Andrews, reprinted by permission of Press Porcepic Limited.

"Lark Song" by W.P. Kinsella: reprinted from *Dance Me Outside* by permission of Oberon Press.

"The Woman and the Wolf" by Farley Mowat: reprinted by permission of McClelland and Stewart.

"Boys and Girls" by Alice Munro: reprinted by permission of McGraw-Hill Ryerson Limited.

"A Sick Call" by Alden Nowlan: from *Miracle at Indian River* by Alden Nowlan © 1968 by Clarke, Irwin & Company Limited. Used by permission of Irwin Publishing Inc.

"Shoes for Dancing" by Geraldine Rubia: reprinted by permission of the author.

"The Skating Party" by Merna Summers: reprinted from *The Skating Party* by permission of Oberon Press.

"The Hanged Man" by Michel Tremblay: reprinted by permission of Intermedia Press.

"Tudor King" by Rudy Wiebe: reprinted by permission of the author.